The Past
Never Dies

The Past Never Dies

A MITCH COOPER Mystery

Bill Craig

ABSOLUTELY AMAZING eBOOKS

ABSOLUTELY AMAZING eBOOKS

Published by Whiz Bang LLC, 926 Truman Avenue, Key West, Florida 33040, USA.

For information contact:
Publisher@AbsolutelyAmazingEbooks.com

ISBN-13: 978-1945772160 (Absolutely Amazing Ebooks)
ISBN-10: 1945772166

To our brave soldiers and sailors on the front lines fighting for our freedom. Your service is appreciated. For the American Flag, long may you wave! And to my children with love...

The Past Never Dies

"The **past** is never dead. It's not even **past**."

- William Faulkner

Chapter One

It was late as Lindsay Call stepped off the curb and crossed the street. Lindsay was a beautiful and curvy brunette with green eyes. Today she was wearing a pale blue pantsuit and heels. She had spent the better part of the day interviewing several high-ranking officers of Micro-Com, a tech company that had just hammered out a huge multi-million deal with China.

Lindsay was a reporter for the San Diego Recorder, an alternative press newspaper. Traffic on the street was light as she headed for her car. One thing that concerned her about the deal was that Micro-Com had agreed to have high-tech computer chips built in China that could possibly allow the Chinese government to gain access to any computer or device that the chips were used in.

The chips would be in anything from cell phones and video games to satellites and ships built for national defense. Lindsay had never trusted the Chinese. Her father had fought in Korea and Vietnam. Both were backed by the Communist Chinese in Beijing.

She was more than convinced that lately, the biggest threat to world peace was not the Russians or Radical Islam, but the Chinese. There were simply too many of them. The Chinese could field more soldiers than any other country on earth. If they could have back doors into American defense computers they would be able to take over without a shot being fired.

She couldn't wait to get home and go over her notes once again so she could start writing the story. Lindsay had just reached her car when she heard the squeal of tires as a car rocketed around the corner and sped towards her. She saw something poking out of the window and dropped to the sidewalk as automatic weapon's fire exploded through the air. Glass shattered and rained down on her and then the car was gone.

Lindsay pulled out her phone and she dialed 911, giving the dispatcher her location. The knee of her pants was torn and bloody. She frowned ruefully as she waited for the cops to get there.

~ ~ ~

Detective Jake Arnold frowned as the car rolled to a stop behind a shot up car outside the offices of Micro-Com. Luke Santos, his partner, whistled between his teeth as he looked at the car and the young woman with the bloodstained pants. "What?" Arnold asked.

"She's good looking, Jake," Santos said, shrugging his shoulders.

"Keep it in your pants, Luke. Let's find out what the hell is going on," Arnold sighed as he opened the driver's door and climbed out of the unmarked car or "slick back" as the detectives called them. Two uniforms were standing off to the side and Arnold sent Santos to talk to them.

"Ma'am, are you okay?" Arnold asked her.

"Sure thing. People shoot at me every day," she rolled her eyes.

"Okay, Lady, we can do this easy or not. I'm giving you the choice," Arnold growled at her.

"I'm the one that got shot at, Detective," Lindsay glared at him with fire in her eyes.

"I can see that, Lady. Can I get your name or is that some kind of state secret?" Arnold sighed. He pulled out a pack of cigarettes and shook one loose. He put it in his mouth and fired it up.

"My name is Lindsay Call. I'm a reporter for the San Diego Reader," Lindsay replied. She watched as the detective frowned.

"A fucking reporter," Arnold shook his head.

"You don't like reporters, Detective?" Lindsay asked.

"Not a whole lot, no," Arnold replied truthfully.

"Somebody in a dark colored car shot at me. Last time I checked, that was a crime," she said.

"I guess. What are you working on?"

"A story."

"That tells me a whole lot, Lady."

"It's what you're getting, Detective," Lindsay said.

"So you tell me," Arnold rolled his eyes.

"I walked to my car and somebody tried to kill me, Detective. That's my statement. I'm going to head for home now," Lindsay told him. She opened the driver's door and brushed the broken glass from the seat and climbed into her car and started the engine. She put the car in gear, driving off and leaving him standing there watching her go.

"Well, shit!" Jake Arnold sighed.

~ ~ ~

Dawn found Mitchell Gary Cooper up and away. He had already stretched and was jogging along the beach. A light fog was coming in off the sea but it was a thermal layer that would burn off in two or three hours. Cooper knew and accepted it. His breathing was slow and easy as he ran, one foot in front of the other.

He wore shorts and a sleeveless sweatshirt as he ran, a .32 Beretta concealed in the pocket of the hoodie. Cooper had never been a man to take chances. He had once been a Navy SEAL and had then worked in Naval Intelligence. Now he was a civilian and a private investigator. He had a small office in a strip mall just outside Coronado. His house wasn't far from there either.

He had managed to build a good sweat this morning as he had run. Many times he saw guys he knew, some of them still active on the teams, but this morning he had not. Today he had been on his own as he had worked his way along the five-mile track that he normally ran.

Cooper was six foot tall and weighed in at about 220. His build was muscular and his daily workout kept him that way. He had blond hair, light blue eyes, and a muscular build. His shoulders were broad and his hips narrow. He had a very close trimmed beard.

Cooper reached his front drive and dropped to a crouch to get his breathing under control. Business was steady enough. He had handled a couple of skip traces and found a teen that had run away and delivered him back to his parents, but other than that it had been a quiet week. The important thing was that the checks had cleared.

His breathing under control again, Cooper entered his home. The house was a single-story ranch style home with an attached two-car garage. Currently, it only held his red Mitsubishi Eclipse, his white GMC Sierra truck was parked outside in the driveway.

A quick shower and he was dressed and ready for the day. He had finally gotten both of his Beretta Px4 Storms back from the San Diego Police Department[1] after they were matched for the self-defense shootings of some Russian spies that had been after one of his clients. One was secured in the gun safe under the seat of his Mitsubishi Eclipse and the other one was now holstered at his waist as he stepped out his front door.

It was barely 8 a.m. but he was ready to start the day. Cooper climbed into the truck and backed out of the driveway heading for the Night and Day Café on Orange Avenue to grab a breakfast that he could take into the office. The fog was burning off quickly and it looked like it was going to be another typical beautiful Southern California day. Another day in Paradise. He grinned at the thought.

Given the average mean temperature was around 75

---

[1] *One More Way To Die*

degrees many would consider it so. Cooper picked up his meal and arrived at the strip mall where his office was located within minutes. The message light was blinking on the machine when he got to his desk. Cooper put his food and coffee down and hit the play button.

"Mr. Cooper, my name is George Rain. I'm the managing Editor at the San Diego Voice and I'd like to discuss hiring you. Please call me back at," and a number was rattled off. Cooper wrote it down and then sat down to eat. Fifteen minutes later, he returned the call.

An efficient sounding woman answered the phone and Cooper told her was returning Mr. Rain's call. She had a nice voice. "One moment, please," she told him.

"George Rain. Is this Mitch Cooper?" asked a gravelly voice.

"Yes, Sir. I understand that you wanted to speak to me," Cooper said, rolling his eyes.

"Could you come over to the newspaper office right away? One of my people needs help. Your name was given to me as someone that could be helpful."

Cooper checked his watch. He didn't really have anything else pressing at the moment. He looked up the newspaper's address on his computer. "Sure, I can be there in about thirty minutes or so."

"Thank you, Mr. Cooper. I appreciate it. I'll see you then," Rain told him before hanging up. Cooper sat back in his chair for a long moment, and then he walked over to a filing cabinet and unlocked it, taking out one of his standard contracts to take with him. He was pretty sure that he was going to be getting a job offer. Relocking the file cabinet, he headed for the door.

~ ~ ~

"Dammit, George, you shouldn't have done that! I don't need a babysitter!" Lindsay Call yelled, her green eyes flashing.

"Sit down and shut up, Call! You may be my best reporter but somebody tried to kill you last night and I had to find about it on television!"

"Okay, I should have called you last night," she sighed.

"You're damn right you should have! How the hell does it look for the paper when one of our reporters is shot at and we get scooped by the TV news! So I don't care if you like it or not, you're getting a bodyguard!" Rain told her.

"What if he doesn't want the job?"

"If so it will be because of your sunny disposition. But from what I was told, he'll take it. You don't have to like it, but you will accept it or you can walk out the door right now and clean out your desk!" Rain snapped.

Lindsay's mouth dropped open. She understood right then how serious that George Rain was about the whole thing. She would either take the protection or lose her job. She swallowed hard. "Yes, Sir," she said meekly.

"What have you got on the story so far?" he asked.

"Enough to make me want to ask a lot more questions. Micro-Com is getting ready to ink a multi-million deal with China to have computer chips built over there. One source, speaking on condition of total anonymity, said that the Chinese were pushing for proprietary ownership of the software, one that would allow them to gain a back door into every system where their chips were used, from cell phones to video games to computers," Lindsay explained.

"Pretty scary stuff," Rain nodded. "Were you able to confirm any of it with any other sources?"

"Yes, Paul Gorman, Chief Executive Officer of Micro-Com and Seth Desmond, an attorney for the World Trade Organization. Both confirmed the deal though I was given the impression that the National Security Agency and Homeland Security were less than happy about the deal."

"So who do you think tried to shoot you last night?"

"I don't know."

"Okay, write up what you have, and then get me a list of what you want to follow up on. When Cooper gets here, I'll make the arrangements and then I'll bring you in to meet him. And Call, be on your best behavior!" Rain ordered.

"Yes, Boss," she said, standing and heading for her desk. At least he hadn't pulled her off the story.

~ ~ ~

Cooper took off his sunglasses as he entered the building. It was one of the many tinted glass monstrosities that had grown up in the city, taking away from the older historical buildings that were the downtown area. A receptionist sat behind a heavy wooden desk that looked almost antique, though the bank of phones and computers on it belied that initial impression. The receptionist herself was a thin redhead with a pixie cut and cool blue eyes, a scattering of freckles across her nose over a Cupid 's bow mouth that promised much. She smiled as he approached.

"Mitch Cooper to see Mister Rain," he told her.

"I'll see if he's available," she replied, giving him just a hint of a smile. He wondered if she was available. She picked up the phone and punched a button, speaking softly for just a moment before hanging up. She looked up at him with luminous eyes. "Take the elevator up to the third floor. Mr. Rain will meet you there."

"Thanks," Cooper told her heading for the elevator. He had to admit, he was curious about why the Managing Editor had called him. Private investigators did not often get called to newspaper offices. Lately, he hadn't done anything that would give them any interest in him for a story, though, he had made the front page a few months ago over the Project Achilles case.[2]

The elevator doors opened and he stepped out onto the third floor. A rumpled looking man with thinning gray hair,

---

[2] *One More Way to Die.*

a pale blue dress shirt with the sleeves rolled up, wearing a gray vest and pants stood there. He figured this had to be George Rain and as soon as the man spoke it was confirmed. "You Cooper?"

"I am," Cooper replied.

"Let's go talk in my office," Rain turned and headed back down the hallway, Cooper trailing behind him.

Chapter Two

Cooper followed Rain down the hall and into a small office. Dingy Venetian blinds allowed some sunlight in through windows that obviously hadn't been washed for a while. Cooper thought that was unusual for a building like this one but didn't say anything. He was more interested in hearing the pitch that Rain seemed to be working himself up to making. The tiles on the ceiling were yellow and smoke stained, a glass ashtray with cigar butts sat on a corner of the desk, showing the man's disdain for the no smoking ban in the workplace.

While Cooper didn't smoke, he did agree that the government was getting way too intrusive in its desire to control the general population and force them to be healthy if they wanted it or not. The way he saw it, if people wanted to kill themselves with smoking cigarettes or cigars, that was their right.

Cooper took a seat across from Rain and looked at the curmudgeonly editor and waited for him to speak. "I've got a reporter that is in trouble."

"So what do you want me for?" Cooper asked.

"She's working on a big story. Last night, somebody took a shot at her. She needs protection," Rain said.

"I'm not a bodyguard," Cooper shook his head.

"But you have done that sort of work before?" Rain asked.

"I have."

"My reporter, she may have uncovered evidence of a Chinese plot to infiltrate the United States military infrastructure and corrupt all of our defense mechanisms to allow for a takeover," Rain said. Cooper sat quietly for a moment, considering.

"Okay, tell me about it," Cooper sighed.

~ ~ ~

Lindsay Call kept shooting glances over at Rain's office.

9

She wondered if that was the guy that Rain had been talking about. He looked fit enough. He might be fun if she wasn't already in a relationship with Sierra. Lindsay had never been one who would cut her dating options in half.

She figured that it wouldn't be long before Rain called her in to meet the guy. She had to admit, he wasn't hard on the eyes. This might not be so bad after all...

~ ~ ~

Chou Chang looked across the desk at Paul Gorman. The American was tall and fit, but his fitness came from a gym rather than through any hard work. "I understand that you spoke with a reporter yesterday."

"I did. She's just a stringer for a local rag. She can't make any trouble," Gorman waived it off.

"I disagree. You don't have too. She must be dealt with. Permanently. Otherwise, the deal is canceled," Chang glared at Gorman.

"Really Chou, you are getting worked up over nothing. I handled her," Gorman said dismissively.

"You answered her questions. This deal was supposed to remain private. By making it public, you have violated the terms of the deal," Chang said softly. His dark eyes found those of Gorman and were unblinking.

"I'll take care of it," Gorman sighed.

"You had better, or I will," Chang replied, rising from his chair. He looked at the American for a long moment, then turned on his heel and walked out of the office.

Gorman watched him go. He picked up his phone and dialed a number from memory. "What happened last night?" he asked.

"I missed." replied the voice.

"Why? You were supposed to take her out," Gorman said.

"She was quicker than I expected," came the reply.

"Kill her. Do it quick," Gorman ordered.

~ ~ ~

10

Chang Chou was incensed! Did Gorman not realize the importance of this deal? It would bring the American a great of money, but it would do far more than that for China! China was already being recognized as a world power, but once the new chips were in use, there was not a single country in the world that would be able to stop them. Gorman was a problem now. One that needed to be removed.

Chou pulled out his phone as he headed for the elevator. He looked at the screen. Not enough signal. He would have to wait until he was out of the building. Perhaps that would be for the best, given the decision that he had made about Gorman.

Minutes later he was out in the hot sunshine walking away from the Micro-Com building, dialing a special number. "Gorman may have exposed us. He talked to a reporter. Eliminate him," Chou said, speaking in his native Chinese.

"Yes," came the reply. Chou headed for his car after hanging up. He needed to get back to the embassy and notify his superiors! He didn't notice the white car that pulled out into traffic behind him. Chang Chou had picked up a tail.

~ ~ ~

"That is a pretty interesting story, Mr. Rain. But does she have any hard proof?" Cooper asked.

"She says she does. She says that there are more people that she needs to talk to," Rain shrugged.

"You think she'll be in even more danger?"

"I do. The thing is, even if I tell her to drop it, Lindsay won't. She's like a bulldog in that once she sinks her teeth into a story, she won't let go of it until it's done."

"Good trait for a reporter. Most of the time. It doesn't sound like this is one of those times."

"I keep telling her that. Still, I'd rather that we break the story than another paper," Rain leaned back in his chair, putting his hands head behind his head.

"You think that will happen?" Cooper asked.

"It will if I try to pull her off of it. She'll just continue to work on it and take it to somebody else."

"Even if it means she might die?"

"Even if. Lindsay is mouthy, sarcastic, and abrasive, but she is the best damn reporter I've ever seen."

"I need two thousand dollars up front for a retainer and after that, it's $500.00 a day plus expenses. I brought one of my standard contracts just in case," Cooper told him.

"You sure you're worth that?" Rain asked.

"Hey, Pal, you called me," Cooper told him, standing up.

"Calm down, Cooper. Give me the contract and I'll sign it, then I'll call down and have a check cut. After that, I guess maybe it's time you meet the young woman you'll be guarding," Rain sighed.

"Sounds like a plan," Cooper nodded. Once the details had been taken care of, Rain stood and walked to the door.

"Call, get in here!" Rain yelled. He stood watching to make sure she was heading for his office before returning to his seat behind the desk. Cooper looked up as the young woman entered. She was easily in at least her early thirties though she didn't look it. She had on a white shell blouse beneath a mint green jacket and mint green slacks. Black heels covered her feet.

"What's up Boss?" Lindsay asked, ignoring Cooper for the moment. It gave him a chance to observe her. He could tell that she had nerve it was obvious in the way that she carried herself.

"This is Mitch Cooper. He's going to be keeping you out of trouble, at least as much as that is possible. My sources tell me that he's a pretty good investigator too. Should you want to utilize him that way," Rain said. Cooper shot the man a look. That was something that had never been discussed.

"I hope he can keep up," Lindsay raised an eyebrow as she looked at Cooper.

"I can keep up," Cooper told her coolly.

"I hope so," Lindsay smiled. Cooper stood and followed her out of Rain's office. Rain trailed along behind them.

"Lady, I haven't exactly agreed to this yet," Cooper told her.

"I hope not. I really don't want a babysitter," Lindsay told him.

"I didn't figure you did."

"So why are you here?" she demanded.

"I'm here because your Boss asked me to be here."

"What if I don't want you to be here?" Lindsay asked.

"I don't give a shit. Your Boss hired me," Cooper replied.

"So you only answer to him?"

"I do."

"Fuck."

"Pretty much. You kiss your mother with that mouth?"

"So what happens now?" Lindsay asked. They both looked at Rain.

"Now you go out and pursue your story and Cooper makes sure nobody kills you," Rain replied

"Whose wheels are we taking?" Lindsay asked.

"Mine," Cooper told her as he stood. Lindsay gave him a resentful look.

~ ~ ~

Chang Chou paced his hotel room. He had just checked his e-mail and the news was less than heartening. His boss was highly displeased with events so far. He took a few moments and swore in Mandarin. The woman was a loose end. One that must be removed. Gorman and his people had been clumsy. Chou's people would not. And to be sure of it, a specialist was on his way sent from Hong Kong. He was known as Lǎohǔ, the Tiger.

Chou had worked with the Tiger before. The man was brutally ruthless and a consummate killer. He was highly skilled in the martial arts and was the Chinese equivalent of a Ninja, also known as a Ghost Walker. The Tiger would eliminate the girl and anyone else necessary.

~ ~ ~

"You expect me to ride around in this?" Lindsay looked at the white GMC pickup with a silver toolbox on the back.

"Yes. It is an anonymous vehicle. It looks like a service truck and nobody in town will even give it a second look," Cooper replied, holding the passenger door for her as she scrambled up into the seat. He closed it behind her and walked around to the passenger door.

"This thing have air conditioning?" Lindsay asked.

"It does, but I rarely use it," Cooper told her as he cranked the engine and backed out of the parking place. He drove to the parking lot entrance and pulled out into the street. "So where are we going?"

"Los Angeles. We need to see the Chinese counsel there."

"Why am I not surprised?"

"I'm not sure, considering we barely met."

"Rain gave me plenty of insight into your personality."

"And what exactly did my boss tell you?" Lindsay half turned in her seat to look at him as Cooper guided the truck north towards highway 101 for the trip.

"He said that you could be an egotistical overbearing bitch, but that you were a damn good reporter. He also said you had a pretty abrasive personality," Cooper told her.

"Sounds like he told you the truth," Lindsay smiled.

"He also gave me a check which I'm depositing before we leave town."

"And you have the nerve to call me mercenary?"

"I'm upfront about what I charge. Can you say the same?" Cooper looked over at her and her cheeks flushed an angry shade of red.

"I have a job to do," Lindsay shot back.

"I do too. Part of it is not letting you throw yourself recklessly into danger."

"Do I have any say about that?"

"Not really, no. Where you go, Miss Call, I go. Get used to the idea."

"What if I don't want to?"

"Then you will probably end up dead."

"Do you really think that?" Lindsay looked at him.

"I do," Cooper replied.

"You are making me a little scared, Cooper. I'm not sure I like that," Lindsay told him.

"You're not supposed to like it, Miss Call. But it is what it is," Cooper told her.

"I'm not sure that you have saved me from anything yet, Cooper."

"If not, then I will. Count on it," Cooper told her. "What are you looking for, Miss Call?"

"I'm looking for truth, Cooper," Lindsay told him.

"What truth is that?" Cooper shot her a glance.

"The truth behind the fact that the Chinese are doing their damnedest to try to take over our country through electronics," Call told him.

"How exactly is that truth?"

"What do you mean, how is that truth?"

"Exactly what I asked."

"You really like semantics don't you Cooper?"

"Is that what you think?"

"Isn't that what it is?"

Chapter Three

The ride to Los Angeles was a long one. "So tell me more about these chips that the Chinese are going to use to take over the world," Cooper said.

"You really want to know?" she looked at him. Shortly after they had started north she had put her hair up in a ponytail to keep it off of her neck and keep herself cooler.

"I wouldn't have asked if I didn't," Cooper replied.

"Most computer chips do nothing more than store or transmit data. How much do you know about computers, Cooper?"

"I know how to turn them on and use them, but I don't know how to write codes for them or anything like that."

"That's what makes these chips different. They actually come with proprietary software built into them. It acts like a Trojan horse almost, allowing the Chinese to take control of the chips and any device that they are embedded in just by sending a simple signal pulse. Micro-Com has caved to the Chinese about the software being built into the chips," Lindsay explained.

"That would be very bad," Cooper agreed. At the first opportunity, he would call Admiral Jason Foster, his "Sea Daddy" from Naval Intelligence and pass the word along. If Foster didn't know about it already. The Old Man was a sneaky one.

~ ~ ~

"Who is this guy again?" Renee Phillips asked as she sipped at her coffee. She looked over at her current partner in her job as liaison officer between the SDPD and NCIS, Special Agent Gabriel King.

"Chang Chou. He masquerades as a businessman when

he's in the United States but he is actually a top lieutenant in the Chinese Black Dragon Tong operating out of Hong Kong," King replied. King sipped at his own coffee. The white Ford LTD that they were sitting in was an older model with a specially modified engine. It was also a good car for stakeouts.

"Why are we on him?" Phillips asked.

"You got something better you'd rather be doing, Phillips?" King asked.

"No, I was just curious."

"Do you remember what killed the cat?"

"I do, but I fail to see how that applies to us sitting here waiting for this guy to come out," Phillips replied.

"We're here because he's suspected of doing a deal that is against the best interest of the United States. He's a known Chinese agent and a criminal as well. Anything else you feel a need to know?" King asked.

"No, I guess that covers it. Being a cop, I just like to make sure that there's good probable cause," Phillips replied sarcastically.

"Good traits for a cop," King agreed.

"Thanks," Phillips rolled her eyes.

~ ~ ~

Cooper found a place to park and escorted the lady reporter towards 440 Shatto Place, the location of the Chinese consulate in Los Angeles. He could tell that Lindsay Call was chomping at the bit, be he also knew that being cautious in their approach would be a more judicious way to handle things. "So what's your plan?" Cooper asked her as they neared the white stone building.

"We go in and I ask to speak to the general counsel, a General Ji Lian. I plan on asking him about the Micro-Com deal and see how he reacts," Lindsay said.

"That's your plan? Hell, you could have done that over the phone," Cooper shook his head.

"In my experience, it is a lot harder to hide a lie when someone is looking you in the face," Lindsay replied. Cooper laughed.

"You really believe that?" Cooper asked.

"I do," Lindsay replied.

"How long have you been a reporter?"

"Ten years."

"You still have a lot to learn. An accomplished liar, and, all of these consulate people are, can lie to your face all day long and you'll never see it," Cooper told her.

"You seem pretty certain of that."

"I used to be in the Navy and I did a stint in Naval Intelligence. I got to know these guys pretty well, and not just the Chinese."

"We'll see."

"I guess we will."

~ ~ ~

San Diego International Airport.

Lǎohǔ stepped off the airplane. He looked around as he left the gate. His was not a big man, standing barely five foot nine. His jet-black hair was shaped to his head and thick black bangs framed his forehead. His almond-shaped eyes were clear and brown as they searched his surroundings, quickly checking for and assessing any possible threats.

The Tiger had landed and he was ready to carry out the job that he had been sent for. A driver was supposed to be waiting for him. Lǎohǔ headed for the baggage claim to get his suitcase. No doubt his driver waited beyond. Chang Chou was not one who was known to be careless or to forget to carry out the proper courtesies. If he had, Lǎohǔ would make sure that he would never forget again.

Lǎohǔ retrieved his suitcase and extended the handle that would allow him to pull the bag behind him as he headed for the exit. Outwardly, he looked serene, but inside he was seething at the insult that had been done to him. He should have been met at the gate. He stepped outside into the afternoon heat. A black liveried driver stood next to a limousine holding a sign with his name written in Chinese characters.

Lǎohǔ didn't bother to speak. He left his suitcase next to the driver and climbed into the vehicle. The driver put his bag in the trunk, then came around and climbed into the driver's seat. Neither of them spoke as the driver pulled the car out into traffic.

~ ~ ~

Detective Jake Arnold climbed out of his car. Luke Santos climbed out the other side and the two of them moved together to the sidewalk and looked up at the glass and steel expanse that was the headquarters for Micro-Com Electronics. The scene looked a lot different than it had the night before. The Crime Scene Unit had swept up all the glass and were turning it into a jigsaw puzzle back at the lab. He had been told they had found a bullet as well. "Looks a lot different in daylight," Luke observed, looking at the way that the clouds reflected off the tinted glass.

"They always do. That reporter said she had been interviewing the top brass. Let's go in and see what they have to say," Arnold replied, heading for the door. Arnold looked as unkempt as ever, his pants wrinkled, his shoes scuffed at the toes and heels, his white dress shirt was dingy from being bleached a few times too many. His tie was nearly at half-mast and stained with food, his jacket flapping around his prodigious middle. His black belt gleamed as did the gold badge that was clipped there just in front of a holster that held a very business-like Glock 17.

Santos was the better dressed of the two in a pale gray tailored suit, over a pale blue dress shirt with a gray tie. His black dress shoes gleamed in the sunlight as they headed for the glass door. Like his partner, Santos wore both his gun and shield on his belt. Santos' Hispanic heritage was obvious in his complexion. He was an up and coming young detective in the San Diego Police Department. But he had a reputation for being cocky. So the Chief had assigned him with Arnold, a borderline racist dinosaur that they were trying very hard to push into retirement.

Surprisingly, the two men from such different backgrounds had hit it off and became a very effective team. Santos was becoming less cocky, and Arnold was actually teaching him how to be a good detective. Their clearance rate was high which made the Chief less likely to boot Arnold out the door yet.

Together the two men pushed through the glass doors and entered the lobby. It was a good ten degrees cooler inside and the sweat that had been running down their faces dried instantly. It was a welcome change. The temperature outside had risen to 80 degrees and the air was humid. A day on the warmer side for San Diego. They stopped in front of a security station, manned by a large uniformed guard that looked like he would be more at home on Muscle Beach. "Can I help you?" the security guard asked.

"Detectives Arnold and Santos to see Mister," Arnold pulled out a notepad and looked at his notes. "Mr. Gorman. San Diego Police Department business."

"I'll call up and see if he's available," the guard said, picking up a phone.

"You do that, Pal," Arnold sighed. He wished he could smoke but knew that it would only result in yet another complaint about him, and that wasn't something he needed. Not with the Chief looking to kick his ass out the door.

"He'll see you. Go to the elevators, take them up to the tenth floor, turn right and go down the corridor. He's the third office on the left," the guard told them.

"Thanks," Arnold said as he started for the elevator, Santos trailing a step behind him. The kid had been busy scoping out the layout.

"It stinks," Santos said.

"What does?" Arnold asked as they reached the elevator and touched the call button to summon it down from wherever it was currently stationed inside the glass and metal behemoth surrounding them.

"There is no way that the security cameras did not catch that shooting outside last night. While he was calling I slipped around behind him. One of the monitors was aimed directly at the place where the reporter's car was parked," Santos said.

"Good news. I wonder if they might be willing to share those tapes."

"They don't use tapes anymore, Jake. Everything is digital these days. But they should have it on DVD."

"So that's what we ask for."

"Indeed it is. So we have a connection between this place and the attempt on the reporter. Might be enough to give us some leverage. Or it might be enough to get us killed."

"You're learning Kid," Arnold told him.

"I suggest we tread carefully here, Partner," Santos suggested as they stepped into the elevator. Arnold stabbed the button for the floor they wanted and the doors slid closed.

"Sounds like a good idea," Arnold agreed. The elevator started to rise.

~ ~ ~

Los Angeles, California.

They were riding upward in an elevator to the third floor. Cooper had been surprised at how easily it had been to get in to see the General. Apparently, the General had been expecting Miss Call. "You call ahead and set up an appointment?" he asked.

"No, I didn't." Lindsay looked worried.

"Seems awful easy."

"Yes, it does."

"Does that worry you?"

"A little."

"Good, stay worried, it may be the edge we need to get out of this alive," Cooper told her.

"You think the General has something planned?" Lindsay looked incredulous.

"You don't?" Cooper asked.

"I don't know."

"Well, you had better make up your mind damn quick."

"I guess so," Lindsay nodded. "Okay, what do we do?"

"If I say move, don't give me any argument," Cooper told her.

"Deal," she whispered. The elevator came to a stop and the door slid open. They stepped outside into the corridor and headed in the direction that they had been given in the lobby.

Soon they came to a door with the General's name spelled out in English. Lindsay stepped forward and knocked. A voice called for them to come in halting English. Cooper opened the door and slid in ahead of Lindsay. Part of her resented it, but another part of her was appreciative. The part of her that resented it, was even more resentful, but at the same time grateful.

Lindsay looked at the small gray-haired man in military uniform sitting behind the desk. "General Ji Lian, how good of you to see us on such short notice," she said.

Chapter Four

General Ji Lian stood as Lindsay moved across the room towards his desk. He smiled warmly at her and extended his hand. Cooper entered behind her, pulling the office door shut behind them. If this was some sort of trap, he wanted at least a little warning.

"Ah, Miss Call, so delightful to actually speak to you in person. I am given to understand you have an interest in the deal between Huian Corporation and your own Micro-Com Corporation," Lian said, his voice smoother than Cooper had expected it to be.

"Yes, General Lian I am. I have some questions about the deal, and the chips in particular," Lindsay smiled at him.

"I am afraid I have no technical understanding about the chips themselves, Miss Call. That is something only the scientists know about," Lian shook his head.

"But can you talk to me about the deal? As to how it came about and what the terms of it are?" Lindsay asked.

"Both of those requests are outside the purview of my position. I only know that a deal was made. As for whatever the terms of said deal might be, they are more of a mystery to me than they are to you," Lian replied.

"General Lian, I have a funny feeling that you are pulling my leg," Lindsay shook her head smiling. Lian frowned, not understanding the meaning of her words.

"I am not touching your leg, Miss Call and I am offended that you would suggest that I would make such an inappropriate gesture!" Lian looked shocked.

"I'm sorry, General Lian. That was just an expression. What I should have said is I don't get the feeling that you are being entirely truthful with me," Lindsay was turning on the charm and doing everything short of batting her long eyelashes at the Chinese General. Cooper rolled his eyes.

"So now you add insults by calling me a liar? Get out now, before I summon security!" General Lian snapped at her, catching her totally off guard.

"Let's go, Lindsay," Cooper said, taking her by the arm and guiding her towards the door.

Out in the hallway, he hurried her towards the elevator. "What the hell, Cooper?" Call asked.

"We need to get out of here and we need to do it now," Cooper snapped. He hit the button and the door slid open. The elevator was empty and Cooper dragged her inside.

"What the hell is going on?"

"He called security, Lindsay. Not just any security, but Chinese troops. Right now we are on Chinese soil so they can't be charged for anything that might happen to us while we are in this building. From the minute we walked through the front door, we have officially been in China for all intents and purposes," Cooper explained.

"Oh!" Lindsay exclaimed.

"That's one way of putting it. Once these doors open, run for the front door. I'll do my best to make sure you get out on the street. If I'm not right behind you, call the cops and then call the Office of Naval Intelligence down in San Diego and tell Admiral Jason Foster what happened. You got that?"

"Got it. Police and then Admiral Jason Foster," she nodded, repeating it to herself. The elevator dinged and the doors slid open. He stepped out, half-dragging Lindsay towards the front door. The guard at the desk stood as they approached.

"Sit!" Cooper snarled at him. The guy threw both hands in the air, after all, he was just a rent-a-cop from some local firm. He wasn't really part of General Lian's staff. The other elevator behind dinged announcing its arrival. Cooper shot a glance over his shoulder and saw the four men in full military uniform charging out of the elevator and drawing weapons. He shoved Lindsay out the front door of the consulate and was only a heartbeat behind her, urging her to hurry towards where his truck was parked.

They were crossing the street when the door to the consulate flew open and the uniformed men stepped out onto the sidewalk, their weapons drawn. An LAPD car that had been passing on the street swung to the curb and the two uniformed officers stepped out to confront the Chinese guards.

Cooper breathed a sigh of relief as he guided Lindsay into his truck. He walked around and climbed into the driver's seat. "I almost got us killed, didn't I?" Lindsay asked.

"Yes, you did," Cooper told her as he pulled out into traffic and began working his way back to the interstate to take them back south to San Diego.

"I'm sorry, Cooper. I should have listened to you," Lindsay told him.

"Yes, you should have. But you didn't. Now, there is a good damn chance that we have a squad of Chinese hitmen on the road behind us somewhere," Cooper told her.

"What are we going to do?"

"I'm working on it," Cooper told her.

"So what have you got so far?" Lindsay looked at him.

"We get the hell back to San Diego," Cooper replied.

~ ~ ~

Paul Gorman looked up as the door to his office opened and his secretary led two men into his office. One was clearly older and looked like a bum; the other was younger and sharply dressed. "Can I help you gentlemen?" he asked.

"I hope so," Jake Arnold said as he dropped unceremoniously into a chair across from the CEO of

Micro-Com.

"You are?" Gorman asked.

"Detective Jake Arnold, SDPD," Arnold replied, flashing his creds at the CEO.

"And your associate?" Gorman asked.

"Detective Luke Santos, also SDPD. Last night a reporter was shot at right outside your offices. We'd like a copy of the security tapes," Arnold said.

"I'll see if we still have them," Gorman smiled smoothly.

"Less than 24 hours, Pal, why wouldn't you have them?" Arnold pushed.

"We record on an 8-hour schedule. After 16 hours, the first 8 hours are erased," Gorman smiled again. Arnold had taken an instinctive dislike to the man. He really wanted to wipe that smug look off of the man's face.

"It's only been about thirteen hours since the time we want. So, the tapes shouldn't have been erased yet," Luke Santos cut in. Arnold felt himself grin at the look of discomfort on Gorman's face.

"Get those tapes for us pronto, Gorman," Arnold said.

"Just as soon as you show me a warrant," Gorman glared at him.

"Luke?" Arnold glanced over his shoulder. Luke Santos reached inside his jacket and pulled out a folded sheet of paper. He handed it to Arnold. Grinning Arnold slid it across the desk to Gorman. "There's your warrant, Pal. Now get us the fucking tapes!"

Glaring at them both, Gorman reached for the telephone and started punching in numbers. "Scotty, burn the surveillance video for yesterday evening and last night onto DVD and bring them to my office. Yeah, the cops are here for them." He hung up. "It'll take about ten minutes," he told them.

"Our techs are top notch people, Gorman. They will be able to tell if the footage had been edited," Arnold told him.

"Kiss my ass," Gorman growled at him.

"You ain't my type," Arnold chuckled. He pulled out his pack of cigarettes and shook one loose, then stuck it in his mouth and fired it up.

"You can't smoke in here," Gorman told him.

"Is that a fact?" Arnold blew smoke at him.

"Anybody ever tell you that you're a total asshole?" Gorman asked him.

"At least once a day," Arnold grinned at him.

"I have to live with him," Santos added, rolling his eyes.

"I feel sorry for you then," Gorman told him.

"Jake, you want to maybe dial it back a notch? Mr. Gorman is cooperating after all," Santos suggested, moving into the role of good cop to Arnold's bad cop.

"Why should I? He may have a fancy office, but he's still a lowlife," Arnold shrugged.

"Why do you have to act this way, Jake? He's trying to help. He wants to know who shot at that reporter too."

"Naw, he doesn't, Luke. He already knows who shot at her. I bet he knows why too," Arnold said, tapping ashes off the end of his smoke onto the polished wood of Gorman's desk. Gorman frowned at him but didn't say anything. They sat and glared at each other until there was a knock on the door.

"Come," Gorman yelled. The door swung open and a uniformed security guard entered the room, two paper sleeves in his hand.

"Here's the video you requested, Sir," the guard said, placing the sleeves holding the two DVDs on the desk.

"You have what you asked for, Detective. Take it and get the hell out of my office," Gorman hissed.

"Thank you for your time and effort," Arnold told him as he scooped the DVD's off the table and carried them towards the door. Santos was right behind him. The uniformed guard stayed behind. Arnold dropped his cigarette on the carpet in the hallway and ground it out with his foot before heading to the elevator. They hit the button and the silver doors slid open. The two cops stepped inside and hit the button for the ground floor. The door closed and the elevator started to sink downward.

"Well-played, Boss," Santos grinned.

"You did good up there, Kid," Arnold told him.

"I learned from the best."

"We'll see, Kid. We'll see."

~ ~ ~

"Who's that?" Phillips asked as the limo pulled up in front of Chou's hotel. King leaned forward in his seat.

"That's a good question," Gabriel King told her.

"You expecting anyone to come calling?" Phillips asked.

"I wasn't, but sometimes things just drop in your lap. You should know that," King replied. Renee didn't say anything because she knew that he was right. More often than not, connections were made on stakeouts when an unexpected visitor arrived. Fortune favored those who waited.

The limo glided to a stop and the driver emerged, stopping to remove a bag from the trunk before moving around to open the rear passenger door. The man that emerged was obviously Asian in appearance. He wore a tailored black suit over a white shirt and black tie. His disdain for his driver was obvious as he headed for the front door of the Hotel, leaving the driver to bring his luggage and follow him.

"His face looked familiar," King mused.

"You know him?" Phillips asked.

"Maybe. Not right off hand, but I've seen his face before," King said.

"In what context?"

"That's what I'm trying to figure out."

~ ~ ~

Lǎohǔ frowned at the elevator. He had a room number and a floor, but his displeasure at being so disrespected was more than evident in his normally inscrutable face. The limo driver had dragged his bag into the elevator and waited stoically behind him. While the man understood his place, he had no idea what the fate that awaited him was. The elevator doors opened and Lǎohǔ stepped out into the hallway. He looked at the door numbers and turned down the direction that he needed to go. The limo driver followed silently.

Lǎohǔ reached Chang Chou's door and rapped his knuckles against it. It took a couple of heartbeats, but Chang Chou opened the door. "Lǎohǔ, it is good to see you," Chou greeted him.

"Are you sure?" Lǎohǔ asked softly.

"I am sure," Chou replied, looking perplexed.

"You need better help," Lǎohǔ told him. His left hand flashed out and the driver lay on the floor, blood flooding from his mouth. He looked at Chou. "I will not be disrespected again."

"None was intended," Chou backed away.

"So you say. The leaders of the Tong are uneasy about your progress."

"I understand. There is a fly that has landed in the ointment. And our associates in this matter have grown sloppy. I need your assistance to clear it up," Chou told him.

Chapter Five

The trip back to San Diego was mostly in silence other than the jazz radio station Cooper had found. "This is big, Cooper," Lindsay Call finally spoke.

"At this point, I have to agree with you. The Chinese normally don't like causing international incidents, but where you are concerned, they seemed willing to risk it," Cooper acknowledged.

"They really don't want my story to get out, which means what I have been saying about the chip all along is the truth!"

"Maybe. Maybe it's all misdirection," Cooper replied.

"Misdirection?" Lindsay turned in her seat to look at him.

"Yes, misdirection. Maybe they want you chasing this story about the microchips when the real story is something different," Cooper explained.

"Like what?"

"I don't know," Cooper replied honestly.

"That's not a big help," Lindsay rolled her eyes.

"I know that. But it is something to think about."

"Maybe."

"I do think that you are right in that it has something to do with the deal with Micro-Com, though," Cooper told her.

"So what kind of deal do you think Micro-Com made with the Chinese?" Lindsay asked.

"I don't know, but I know we won't find out in Los Angeles."

"I don't know the name of the Chinese rep working on the deal, but I did get a picture of him."

"Do you have it with you?"

"No, it's back at the office."

"I need to see it. I might know some people who can put a name to his face."

"Who?" Lindsay asked suspiciously.

"A friend in Naval Intelligence."

"And they will just check the face for you in facial recognition?"

"Yes."

"Who the hell are you, Cooper? You're not just another keyhole peeper," Lindsay shook her head.

"Before I left the Navy I worked in Naval Intelligence," Cooper replied.

"Why am I not surprised?" Lindsay rolled her eyes.

"I have no idea," Cooper grinned at her, "Especially since I mentioned it once before."

~ ~ ~

They drove for a while in silence before Lindsay broke the silence. "I've been thinking about what you said. About the misdirection. I'm trying to figure out what else could be going on besides this stuff with the chip. Do you have any ideas?" she asked.

"Maybe. Do you know where the chips are being manufactured?" Cooper asked.

"All that stuff is back at the office," Lindsay shook her head.

"Do you mind letting me take a look at it when I get you back?"

"Before, oh hell no. But now, you might actually be useful."

"I'm glad you think so."

"What can I say, Cooper; you won me over."

"If I did it's only temporary I'm sure."

"You don't trust me?"

"Think about that for a minute."

"Okay, I get it. Call it a temporary truce then."

"That I can buy," Cooper told her.

"I thought you might."

~ ~ ~

They had reached San Diego and Cooper threaded his way back to the newspaper office. Lindsay Call was actually quiet for once. Cooper glanced over at her and saw that her expression was tense. "What?" he asked.

"You make me nervous, Cooper. You with your government connections. I have to ask myself, how far can I trust you?" Lindsay said.

"You can trust me to keep you alive when the Chinese come after you and come after you they will. You've found something that they don't want to be made public. They seem more than ready to kill to keep it a secret."

~ ~ ~

Two hours later they were back at the newspaper. Lindsay had proved more than willing to show Cooper her notes now that she was sure he was on her side. He had spent time reading all of the documentation and by the time he was finished Cooper agreed with her conclusions.

"This is big," Cooper told her.

"I'm glad you agree," she told him.

"Have you alerted the authorities?"

"I don't have enough proof yet."

"It's enough for me."

"But not enough for the proper authorities."

"You've approached them already?

"I have."

"Let me try," Cooper told her.

"So have at it. See if it does any good," she waved her arms.

~ ~ ~

"Tell me more about this fly," Lǎohǔ said. The driver was slowly picking himself up off the floor. He glared at his former passenger but knew better than to say anything. He departed the room quickly and silently.

"Our contact at Micro-Com spoke to a reporter. One Lindsay Call. He feels that she can cause no difficulty to our operation, but I am not so sure," Chang Chou said.

"Why?"

"She is a reporter, and the reporters here cannot be as easily controlled as the ones in our homeland. Americans are far too trusting of their so-called free press than our government."

"So what do you want done?"

"I want her removed as quickly as possible and her story shut down. It is hard telling how much that fool, Gorman revealed to her about our new microchips. We cannot let the Americans know that with them we will be able to disable their entire defense network!"

"Do you know where I can find her?" Lǎohǔ asked softly.

"Here is the address of the newspaper that she works at," Chou slid a small slip of paper with the address scribbled on it across his desk.

"I will take care of it," Lǎohǔ told him. He stood and turned away, calling over his shoulder," You will see that my bags are placed in my room."

Chang Chou watched the deadly assassin leave, the door shutting behind him. He collapsed in his chair. Sweating freely now that Lǎohǔ was no longer in the room. While he was a high-ranking member of the Black Dragon Tong, the Tiger frightened him like no other man on earth. Based on the stories that he had heard, Chou was not totally sure that Lǎohǔ was entirely human!

~ ~ ~

Renee Phillips had watched as the driver came out of the hotel and drove away. He looked a little worse for wear to her, blood leaking from swollen lips. Apparently, he had done something to anger his passenger and reprisals had happened inside. She glanced over at King but his dour expression remained the same giving nothing away about whatever was going on in his head.

"Any closer to figuring out who that guy was?" she asked.

"Not yet, but it will come to me," King replied.

"You don't talk a lot do you?"

"Nope."

"Why is that?"

"I've learned that most people don't like silence. Most of them feel obligated to fill it up. The more they talk, the more they reveal," King shrugged.

"Interesting."

"Is it?"

"It is to me," Phillips replied.

"Why is that?" he asked, knowing that she had some underlying motive for her comment.

"Because you don't like to reveal much about yourself. What exactly are you hiding, Agent King?" Phillips asked.

"Are you sure that is a question you really want to know the answer to?" he looked over at her.

"It is. I like to know the people I am working with."

"Like you knew Cooper?"

"I wasn't actually working with him. But I trusted him."

"Right," King rolled his eyes.

"You say that like it's a bad thing."

"Maybe because I know a hell of a lot more about Mitch Cooper than you do," King shook his head.

"How is that?" Phillips looked at him expectantly.

"You know Cooper used to be a Navy SEAL, right?"

"Yes. I also knew that he was in Naval Intelligence afterward."

"Yeah well when he was a SEAL he got involved in some sketchy stuff. Stuff that I had to look into. Cooper came up clean, but not all of his men. Then I used one of his agents, a young woman on a case to infiltrate a gang. It didn't end well for the agent. The gang members responsible all died. I'm sure that Cooper took them out, but I could never find the evidence to prove it," King told her.

"And that bothers you," it wasn't a question.

"It does. Nobody is above the law, Phillips."

"Not even you?"

"Not even me."

"Then why, if you'll pardon me asking, aren't you dead too? I mean if Cooper blamed you for his agent's death?"

"I ask myself that question every day," King admitted.

"Seems to me that Cooper isn't the one with the problem, Agent King."

"Hey, you asked," King shrugged dismissively.

"I did. So you don't like Mitch Cooper and he doesn't like you. Yet you can work together when you need to."

"We can. It's more about respect than anything else. Cooper knows me, and I know him. We may not like each other, but we respect each other."

"That's something."

"I guess."

"So why do you dislike the fact that I trust Cooper?"

"Because I think you are a fool for doing so," King told her.

"Jake Arnold felt the same way."

"Your old partner on the SDPD?"

"Yes," Phillips replied.

"He was an asshole."

"He still is."

"But he didn't like Cooper either?"

"Nope."

"Maybe I misjudged the son of a bitch," King said.

"No, you didn't," Phillips told him.

~ ~ ~

Mitch Cooper frowned as he read the notes that Lindsay Call had put in front of him. From what he had read so far, he had a feeling that she was correct in her assessment about the Chinese built microchips. He looked up at where she sat on the other side of the table. "You are totally sure about this and its accuracy?" he asked.

"I am. I have spent a lot of time on this story, Mr. Cooper. I verify everything before I ever consider putting it in print," Call told him.

"Okay, you do good work, Call. What you have uncovered is big, and it could set not only the computer industry but the military on its collective ear!"

"I told you," Lindsay sat back with a self-satisfied smirk on her face.

"Yes, you did. The thing is, you've also painted a target on your back. The Chinese can't let this come to light. If it does, it will set back U.S./Chinese relations a long way. And that can also be problematic since they own a lot of the United States Debt," Cooper told her.

"You believe that they will come after me?"

"I do. And I think that they know that they need to silence you. No matter what," Cooper told her.

"Oh," Lindsay said quietly.

Chapter Six

"What do we do now?" Lindsay Call asked.

"First thing we need to do is get you someplace safe and out of the way," Cooper replied, his tone all business.

"How can I pursue this story if we do that?"

"Do you want to die, Miss Call?"

"No."

"If you keep pursuing this story, you very likely will. I don't want to be collateral damage," Cooper told her.

"You turning chicken on me Mr. Bodyguard?" Lindsay rolled her eyes in disgust.

"Not at all. I just want to keep you safe. But I can't do that if you insist on making a target of yourself. I can put you somewhere safe and continue to investigate, but I can't do both."

"How will it still be my story if I'm not the one looking into it?"

"Because I will share with you everything that I find. I give you the details, you write the story," Cooper told her.

"Let me think about it," Call told him.

"How long do you need?"

"How about overnight?"

"I'll give you that, but you go to a safe house for the night. Not home. That is unconditional."

"What about clothes?"

"We'll stop and buy you some for tomorrow."

"Okay," Lindsay Call agreed.

Jake Arnold sipped at his coffee as he watched the DVD of the attack on Lindsay Call at Micro-Com. Luke Santos was watching over his shoulder. "Okay, we know that the folks at Micro-Com lied to us about not seeing the shooting. The security guard had to have seen it," Santos said.

"Yeah he did, and that son of a bitch in charge had to know it too. What was his name again?" Arnold asked.

"Ed Gorman," Santos replied with a grin.

"We need a warrant to see what the fuck else that asshole is hiding," Arnold said.

"I'll see what I can do," Santos told him. Jake Arnold leaned back in his chair and sipped at his coffee. It was cold but he drank it anyway. He had a bad feeling about Gorman, the guy at Micro-Com. He was dirty as hell. All Arnold had to do was prove it. That part might actually be fun!

~ ~ ~

"Any idea who this guy is, yet?" Phillips asked as they followed a yellow cab into the suburbs.

"Not yet, but I'm sure it will come to me," King replied. He never took his eyes off the target vehicle that carried the unknown Chinese agent.

"I hope you'll let me know when it does," she told him.

"I will."

"What put you onto Chang Chou?" Renee asked.

"Aside from the fact that his passport is flagged to let us know anytime he comes into the United States?"

"Yeah, aside from that."

"I busted him once in Hong Kong. It didn't stick, of course, The Black Dragon Tong bailed him out. But it brought him to my attention. He was running drugs back then, selling them to Sailors and Marines on leave. I'm not sure what he's running now, but I know for damn sure that it is likely illegal," King shrugged.

"So we are following this guy on a hunch?"

"Pretty much. It seems likely that he's working for Chang Chou which means that he's up to no good."

"Says who?" Phillips looked at him.

"My gut," King told her.

"Your gut? Are you sure that's admissible in court?"

"Nope, but it's good enough for me."

~ ~ ~

Mitch Cooper used his credit card to purchase whatever Lindsay Call might need over the next few days. He held onto the receipt to bill it to the paper under expenses. Her boss had been right, she was something of a feisty fireball, but that was okay. It meant that she might well have a chance of surviving if he could get her to listen to reason.

So far she had agreed to co-operate with him, but he knew ahead of time that was a slippery slope. That he couldn't trust her not to run was a given. Still, he liked her. She had both gumption and moxie like he hadn't seen in a long time. One of the last of the old-time journalists; training wise anyway. He knew a bunch that would have cut and run by this point. But not Lindsay Call. So he was in for the long haul, protecting her until she had filed the story.

They carried everything out to his truck and piled it in, and then he drove her to one of several safe houses that he had set up throughout the city. All of the safe houses were equipped with WIFI so that she could continue to work and file her stories to the paper.

The Chinese connection bothered him. It bothered him a lot. He needed to find out more about it. He needed to know about the company that was actually manufacturing the computer chips and where they were located. Cooper was beginning to get a bad feeling about it all.

According to what he had read in her notes, the chips were being manufactured by Huawei Technologies. Cooper needed to know where their Chinese plants were located. It was a ghost from his past, one that he had hoped to bury and leave forgotten. Except now it was coming back, rearing up like the ugly head of a hydra.

~ ~ ~

China, 1995.

Mitch Cooper looked up over the edge of the ditch, his blue eyes scanning for guards. Sweat was beaded on his brow, causing the camouflage make-up that covered his face to run a bit. A do-rag covered his close-cropped hair. He glanced over his shoulder at his team. They were all ready.

This was a covert insertion to disrupt a factory that was supposedly manufacturing computer chips that somebody back in D.C. had decided were dangerous to the United States security. The plan was to demolish the building, grab a sampling of the chips and then get the hell out without being discovered.

His SEALs he knew were up for the job. IF they had been given the proper intelligence from Washington to do what they were supposed to do. Cooper knew that was a damn big if. Too often lately the Intel that his team was being given was sketchy at best...

~ ~ ~

Cooper pulled himself back to the present. He hated when he had flashbacks, but the Shrink he saw on a semi-regular basis assured him they were normal. Cooper wasn't so sure. For the most part, he had adjusted pretty well to civilian life, but there were times...

Now wasn't the time, he told himself, shutting down all thoughts of Post-traumatic Stress Syndrome. It was something that every soldier suffered from. Back in the day, they had called it battle fatigue or shell shock. Cooper didn't know a single soldier or sailor that had been in a battle that didn't suffer from it. Especially SEALs.

He pulled out his cell phone and dialed the Admiral. Admiral Jason Foster answered on the first ring, almost as if he had been expecting Cooper's call. Cooper knew that wasn't possible but it still made the small hairs on the back of his neck stand on end.

"What can I do for you, Mitch?" Foster asked

pleasantly.

"Maybe I can do something for you," Cooper told him.

"That would certainly be a pleasant surprise."

"I have a client that seems to have uncovered some conspiracy between the Chinese and an American company to flood the market with a computer chip that allows the Chinese to backdoor into every American computer that they are installed in."

"You have my attention," Foster told him.

"Good," Cooper said.

"So talk, Cooper," Foster commanded.

"The Chinese have struck a deal with Micro-Com to make chips for them. What Micro-Com isn't telling is that the Chinese have proprietary software on the chips that gives them access to any computer, phone, or gaming device that they are implanted in. Basically, it can allow them to take control of those devices at anytime they see fit, not to mention using them to mine information on the devices," Cooper explained.

"That has National Security implications," Foster said.

"Yes, it does. How do you want me to handle it?" Cooper asked.

"Keep digging. The more information we have, the better to turn it around and bite the Chinese on the ass with it."

"That's what I figured."

"Good. Anything that we can do to cause them embarrassment is a good thing. They have been flexing their muscles just a little too much of late. It's time to shut them down."

"And you think this can?"

"It can if it gets made public. I'm counting on you to make that happen."

"I'll see what I can do," Cooper hung up. He frowned as he considered what he had learned.

Cooper wondered if he would be able to talk Call into going along with what he had planned. He hoped that he would. "A friend has given me the go-ahead to help you make this deal as public as possible."

"Is that a good thing?" Lindsay asked.

"For the most part," Cooper told her.

"So it is a good thing."

"I guess."

"You don't sound all that certain," she observed, tilting her head to the right as she looked at him.

"I don't like dangling you out as bait to draw the Chinese out. It's dangerous as hell for you," Cooper told her.

"Why Cooper, I'm beginning to think you might actually care," Call rolled her eyes.

"I'm getting paid to care," he replied, shrugging his shoulders. She had proven to be a damn good investigator, but she was impulsive and that impulsiveness could get her killed if she wasn't careful.

Despite himself, Cooper found that he kind of liked her in spite of her rather abrasive personality. He shook his head slightly. It appeared that she was growing on him. Like an unwanted fungus. He doubted that she would appreciate the comparison.

He left Call to set up her computer and went into the kitchen to make dinner. He kept the larder in each of the safe houses fully stocked because he never knew which one that he might be using at any given time. And he did spend time in them, given that some of his clients were high-profile tech people or former Navy officers. Sometimes even some of his old buddies from the teams or ONI. He made it a practice to never use the same one two times in a row.

While enemy agents might set up on one, if he never went there, they would eventually lose interest and write it off as a wrong address. He had surveillance systems set up on each property and if one appeared to get too much attention, he would simply list it with a broker, sell it and then go to a different broker and buy a new one.

~ ~ ~

Gabriel King frowned as the car they were following drove past the offices of one of the many smaller newspapers that dotted the San Diego area. It had appeared to take a special interest in that particular building and he couldn't help but wonder why. He glanced over at Phillips and saw that she had noticed it too, though she had yet to mention it. She was learning.

The car circled the building twice, getting a lay of the land so to speak, and then it headed back towards the hotel. King stayed with it.

"I wonder what that was all about," Phillips said.

"Not exactly what I had expected to happen either," King told her.

"What did you expect?"

"I don't know, but that wasn't it."

"Do you have any idea why this Chou guy is doing in town?"

"Not really, no."

"Do you think maybe we should try to find out?"

"I think that might be a really good idea, Phillips," King told her, never taking his eyes from the vehicle that they were following.

"I do too, King."

"Any thoughts?"

"Maybe somebody at the paper learned something that Chou doesn't want to be made public?"

"There might be hope for you yet," King grinned.

Chapter Seven

Lindsay Call lay under the sheets. The bedroom windows were open to allow in what little breeze came in from the sea. A small fan whirred on the dresser, sending cool air washing over her. She was having trouble sleeping and it was because of the story. She realized that she had nearly gotten both Cooper and herself killed at the Chinese consulate up in Los Angeles. As much as she hated the idea, she had to start trusting Cooper. He knew what he was doing and he had proven that to her over and over.

Still, it was a hard thing for her to do. She was used to being a strong and independent woman, one who never had to rely on anyone else to get the job done. Except for this time, she did need to rely on Cooper to keep her safe so she could get the job done. At least he hadn't tried putting any moves on her. While she appreciated it, it was almost depressing. Was she losing her appeal? She smiled at that and then shook her head.

Not likely. It had more to do she was sure, with Cooper being a consummate professional. He had that air about him. An aura of supreme confidence and knowledge that he was very good at what he did.

She had looked him up earlier while he was making them dinner. He was everything he had said, a former sailor and decorated Navy SEAL, and then intelligence operative for Office of Naval Intelligence. He had been working as a private investigator and security consultant since leaving the navy and he had a lot of important people that were grateful for the work he had done for them. He had even managed to break up a Russian spy ring a couple of months back.

There was a lot more to Mitch Cooper than what showed on the surface. He was more than some beach bum surfer type. He had, what was the word? Substance, yes, that was the word. He had substance to him. He had saved her life earlier. She was pretty sure of that. She closed her eyes. She needed to sleep because tomorrow was going to be a busy day.

~ ~ ~

Mitch Cooper had his own laptop going in the living room downstairs. His Beretta PX-4 Storm lay on the coffee table beside it. Admiral Foster had seemed a little too eager to give the go ahead to this particular venture. That made Cooper nervous, though he would never let Call know that.

Anytime the Admiral was overly helpful was suspect as far as Cooper was concerned. Foster was a friend, and his former "Sea Daddy" back when he was on the teams. But he also ran the Navy's top spy agency. Foster had used him in the past and Cooper was pretty damn sure that Foster would use him again in the future. There wasn't much he could do about it, but he could be cautious enough not to take it at face value. So anything Foster gave him was suspect as far as Cooper was concerned.

The whole microchip thing bothered him. It brought back memories of a mission that had been sabotaged years in the past. They weren't supposed to succeed. He had lost men because of it. He still owed whoever had blown their mission. Haynes, Miller, Canales, Kowalski. They had all lost their lives, and it had been for nothing. The whole thing was nothing but an elaborate trap. Cooper had been sure afterward that the whole team had been supposed to die, but they hadn't. He had managed to get the rest of his team out.

It wasn't long after that when he had left the teams to go into intelligence. He had lost too many men to bad Intel, and he had not wanted that to happen again.

He picked up the bottle of Killian's Red sitting next to the computer and took a long pull from it. His favorite beer. Cooper rarely drank anything stronger, but sometimes he did. Tonight was not the night for whiskey. No, he was sure that the Chinese would be coming after them. That was why they had come to the safe house. He didn't want them to try for them at his home. It wasn't much, but it was where he lived. He stood and stretched and then walked over and turned on the CD player. The Beach Boys began to sing about a little surfer girl. The music of Southern California. He took another pull at his beer and returned to his seat.

~ ~ ~

Lǎohǔ had the driver take him back to the motel. He now knew where the paper was located. He could find it again when he drove there on his own. It would not be a difficult task to break in and find out exactly what the newspaper reporter knew.

That would determine his future course of action. Depending on what he found, the woman might well need to die. He had no qualms about it if she did. His job was to keep the true purpose of the chips from becoming public. The Black Dragon Tong was a strong one in China, and they were his lord and master. Chang Chou was nothing more than an insect that he would squash if he outlived his usefulness.

Lǎohǔ headed back upstairs to his room to rest. He would require all of his energies to deal with what he found later. He would deal with Chang Chou later. It would not be pleasant for the other man.

~ ~ ~

"So what exactly did we learn?" Phillips asked as King parked in the motel lot.

"We learned that this fucking mystery man is interested in something at that fish-wrapper of a newspaper. That seems like a lot," King shrugged.

"How so?" Phillips asked.

"It's more than we knew before."

"So it is. But what exactly does it tell us?"

"It tells us that the newspaper is on to something that the Black Dragon Tong doesn't want to be made public."

"Any idea what that might be?" she looked over at him.

"Nope, but it's more than we had before."

"According to your gut?"

"Of course."

"How often does the court system trust your gut?"

"They don't, not until I've made a case," King replied.

"I see."

"No, you don't. Right now, Phillips, you are still thinking like a San Diego cop. I've been chasing spies for years. They aren't like regular criminals and sometimes you have to think and act outside the box to catch them," King told her.

"I'm beginning to see that. So what exactly do you expect us to do?" Phillips asked.

"We stay on the son of a bitch until he steps out of line," King shrugged.

~ ~ ~

They had climbed out of the ditch and made their way to the wall of the factory. Cooper had sent Canales and Kowalski ahead to check the outside door. It was unlocked. They gathered beside it. Cooper looked around at each man. They all knew their jobs, knew what was required of them. They were ready. He nodded and Kowalski was the first one through the door...

~ ~ ~

Mitch Cooper blinked away the memory. Now wasn't the time for it. Except he had to know the name of the company that was making the computer chips. Call had printed out all of her notes and they were in a manila folder. Cooper opened the file and started to read.

It took about an hour before he found the name of the company that was producing the chips. It was a familiar one. It was the same company that owned the plant that his team had raided back in the day.

Cooper frowned as the memories tried flooding back into his mind. He pushed them away. He was sweating and his hands were shaking. He took a deep breath and let it out slowly.

~ ~ ~

He had followed Kowalski inside. The plant was dark and quiet as his men entered and spread out. They each had specific objectives. Cooper knew that. He had a bad feeling about it. It felt like a setup. Cooper clicked his comm, calling his men back. He had personally grabbed a handful of the chips and stuffed them into a bag. "Let's get the hell out of here!" he told his men. They started out of the building and that was when everything went to hell in a handbasket

~ ~ ~

Cooper blinked his eyes. He looked at his watch. Nightmares. China had certainly been a place for them. He had the scars to prove it. Both physical and mental. It wasn't something he wanted to revisit again tonight. Cooper grabbed his pistol and walked around the house, making sure all the doors were locked. Windows too. He silently opened Call's door. She had the window open a little. Cooper silently cross the room and closed and locked it. The central air was working and was set at 68 degrees. The room was cool enough. He slipped out and headed to his own bedroom.

Once inside he stripped down to his skivvies and sat down on the bed. He pulled out a book, *The Unfinished Conversation* by Evangeline Thiessan. It has some interesting points that he was thinking of adding to his own research on the matter of Cosmic Connections and Cosmic sex. Cooper turned on the bedside lamp before turning out the overhead light. He walked back to the bed and lay down and before long, he was asleep.

~ ~ ~

Lǎohǔ had slipped out of the hotel, merging with the shadows of the night and made his way to a rental car that he had ordered Chang Chou to procure and leave for him at a designated spot. He had spotted a tail earlier in the day and he wanted to make sure that whoever it was, was not following him tonight. Lǎohǔ had private business to attend to, and it was a business that he wanted no witnesses to. He found the keys in the glove compartment and inserted them into the ignition, starting the car and driving towards his objective.

The newspaper offices were dark as he drove past. That was good. With luck, The Tiger could be in and out with no one being the wiser. He needed to locate the reporter. She had not been at her home. Chang Chou had checked. She was a loose end that needed to be removed as soon as possible. With her dead, the story would end and the American government would be none the wiser of what the Black Dragon Tong had managed to accomplish. Not until it was too late.

He parked the car on a side street and made his way to the newspaper office. The lock was an easy one to defeat and within seconds he was inside. A security guard snoozed at his desk. Lǎohǔ slipped easily past him without disturbing him.

The Tiger glided past the elevators and elected to take the stairs. This way if the elevators made a noise, it would not alert the sleeping guard. He eased the door shut behind him and glided up the stairs. He had noted the location of the floor of the newsroom from the directory below.

Lǎohǔ entered the newsroom. He could read English and quickly found the cubicle belonging to Lindsay Call. He booted up her computer but was surprised to learn that it was password locked. He searched her desk for the password with no success. Lǎohǔ frowned angrily at the computer before shutting it down. This reporter was much smarter than the journalists in his own country. Most of them kept a written record of their passwords. It was obvious that the Call woman did not. It was not an insurmountable obstacle, however.

There was a lot of trash in her wastebasket. He produced a lighter and ignited some of the papers in it after pouring them out around her computer. The flames would destroy any evidence stored there. As the flames caught, The Tiger disabled the fire alarms. With luck, the entire building would be destroyed! Then he vacated the premises.

The drive back to the hotel was a quick and quiet one and he managed to enter once more without being seen. The Tiger frowned because his mission to the United States had just become a whole lot more complicated.

~ ~ ~

Jake Arnold frowned as he watched the firefighters try to put out the blaze that had erupted within the offices of the San Diego Reporter. He wasn't buying an accident. Not after reading the latest report from Lindsay Call about the Micro-Com deal. He had a feeling that the Chinese were behind the fire, and they had hoped that the lady reporter would be caught up in it.

Santos walked up carrying two cups of coffee. "Think this is related?" Santos asked, referring to the earlier attempt on Lindsay Call's life.

"Damn straight I do. The lady reporter seems to have stumbled into something big," Arnold sighed.

"Any idea where we might find her?"

"Not yet. But I have a pretty good idea who to ask," Arnold told him.

Chapter Eight

Mitch Cooper snapped awake when his cell phone started to ring. He snatched it up off of the nightstand. "Cooper," he said.

"Somebody torched the offices of The San Diego Recorder tonight," Admiral Foster's voice filled his ear.

"What?" Cooper asked, trying to wake up and get himself oriented.

"Isn't that where the reporter you are working with works?"

"It is. You think it's because of the story?"

"You don't?"

"On the surface yes, but what is the end game?"

"Clearly the Chinese don't want her story coming out. I have to ask myself why? Seems like a question you should be asking too."

"Believe me I am. I'm thinking this might have something to do with one of my old missions when I was with the teams," Cooper replied softly.

"The one where..." Foster let it hang.

"Yeah, that one."

"I see. I'll pull the file. I'm sure you'll want to come in and review it?" Foster asked.

"Yeah, I will. There were too many things that went wrong on that mission to be a coincidence. And now, a decade later, it seems to be popping up again."

"Despite what people might think, Mitch, the past never dies."

"So I'm finding out," Cooper replied.

"Come in as soon as you can."

"Aye, Aye Sir," Cooper replied breaking the connection.

He stood. He should let Lindsay know what had happened. He headed down the hallway and knocked lightly on her door. It took a moment or two before her sleepy voice called for him to come in. Cooper took a deep breath, let it out and turned the knob and stepped inside.

~ ~ ~

Renee Phillips answered the phone. She had been in a deep sleep and was still groggy. "Hello?"

"Get dressed and meet me out front. Somebody just burned down the newspaper offices that the Chink was checking out earlier," King told her.

"Give me five minutes," Phillips said before hanging up the telephone. She sat up and threw aside the blanket and satin sheets she had been sleeping on. Once her feet hit the floor, her mind was already racing and full of questions. She made her way to the bathroom and took care of business before getting dressed in a dark blue pants suit with a white blouse. Her Glock was holstered on her hip before she stepped into her shoes and headed out the door. She hoped King had either brought coffee or would stop for some. Being rolled out in the middle of the night she needed it.

Gabriel King looked as fresh as could be as she slid into the passenger seat beside him. The car was moving before she managed to get the door shut and her seat belt buckled. "Coffee?" she asked.

"Center console," King said. Phillips gratefully picked up the cup and took a sip. It was hot but that was good. The caffeine gave her a jolt that helped her assemble her thoughts in a working order.

"Was it arson?" she asked.

"Appears to be."

"You think the guy that Chang Chou imported did it?"

"He's as good a suspect as anybody," King replied as he guided his car through the streets.

"So what are we going to do?"

58

"We are going to insert ourselves into the investigation and see what we can shake loose."

"You think we'll find something?"

"I think we will. The reporter seemed to be on to something."

"Do we know what it was?"

"Nope, but I think Mitch Cooper might know," King replied.

"Why is that?" Phillips asked.

"Because the newspaper hired him to protect the girl while she worked on her story.

"Why is that?"

"I don't know yet, but I intend to find out."

"But you don't know?"

"No, I don't. But even I can connect the dots."

"This isn't part of your personal grudge against Cooper is it?" Phillips asked.

"Not this time."

"Do you know where to find him or the reporter?"

"Not yet. But I will. I want to look at the crime scene first."

"Okay," Phillips nodded.

~ ~ ~

"What do you mean burnt down?" Lindsay Call demanded.

"I was told the place was torched and it seemed to start in your cubicle. That seems to imply somebody was after you," Cooper told her.

"It does. Cooper, I'm scared," Lindsay said.

"You should be. Somebody wants you dead and they want this story buried," Cooper told her.

"I get that."

"I hope so, Lindsay. Because this is some serious shit that you are involved in," Cooper told her.

"I know that," Lindsay looked down at the sheets that

covered the lower part of her body.

"I hope so. Because it is time you started taking this seriously," Cooper told her. "I can't protect you if you aren't willing to do what I tell you when I tell you. I'll help you dig as much as I can, but keeping you safe until this story is published is what I was hired to do."

"I get it Cooper, I really do. It's hard for me, you know? I've worked like a dog to get where I am. I've done it on my own. Nobody ever helped me in the past. That's why I am like I am. I'm used to doing things on my own."

"Well, that has to change. I can't keep you from getting killed if you try to do this on your own."

"I know. Thank you, for what you've done for me so far."

"You're welcome. Try to get some more sleep. I'll wake you up in a couple of hours for chow and then we can figure out a plan of action for the day."

"One that doesn't include getting either one of us killed?"

"Especially that," Call smiled at him. Cooper smiled back and walked out of the room, shutting the door behind him. Cooper made a quick check of all the doors and windows before returning to bed. He hoped that he could believe her.

Cooper lay down and pulled the sheets over his body and closed his eyes, trying to shut down his mind and return to a restful slumber. Soon he was fast asleep.

~ ~ ~

The news about the newspaper office being burned down was all over the airways the following morning. It was the lead story on the morning news cycle and it would run there for most of the day. Cooper had turned the television on when he had come downstairs to start cooking breakfast.

He could hear Call moving around upstairs as he set about cooking bacon and then frying eggs in the grease. The toast popped from the toaster as she emerged in the kitchen. Call grabbed them out of the toaster and carried them to the table to butter and then spread strawberry jam over them. She put two more slices in the toaster and got a glass from the cabinet and poured herself some orange juice. She drank it and put the glass in the sink and grabbed a coffee mug and filled it up as Cooper moved the eggs from skillet to plates. The bacon was already on the table atop a paper towel on a plate. Cooper already had his own cup of coffee.

"You're still here," he noted.

"Did you expect me to sneak out a window and shimmy down the gutter during the night?" Lindsay asked.

"I'm not sure exactly what I expected of you, Call. But I'm glad you're still here. It means you actually listened when I woke you up," Cooper shrugged. He took a seat and grabbed a slice of toast to add to the eggs on his plate, followed by a few strips of bacon. He sipped his coffee.

"I gave you my word. It's pretty much all I have that's worth anything," Call shrugged.

"That's good enough for me," Cooper told her.

~ ~ ~

Gabriel King was the first one in the office. He dropped into his chair and snatched up the phone. He dialed Admiral Jason Foster's personal extension.

"Hello?" the Admiral's voice filled his ear.

"Admiral Foster, Gabe King, NCIS. I'm looking for Mitch Cooper. Any idea where I might find him?" King asked.

"Why?" Foster asked.

"Admiral," King replied.

"Do you have a problem with Cooper, Agent King?"

"Maybe. But if I do, it's between me and him."

"How can I be sure of that?"

"You have my word on it."

"What if that isn't enough?"

"What do you mean by that?"

"It means I don't trust you, Agent King. Even if Cooper does. You are on your own this time."

"I usually am," King sighed as the line went dead. He looked at the handset and gently put it back in the cradle. Whatever the hell was going on, it went way up the chain of command, high above his pay grade. Did he really want to delve into that particular can of worms? He needed to think about that as he waited for the rest of his team to come into the office.

~ ~ ~

Admiral Foster sat back in his chair. This case was getting out of control. His agents were playing fast and loose with the rules, and because of that, there were good people that might get killed. He didn't want that to happen. Mitch Cooper had been like a son to him, and the kid had a real talent for investigation. There was no way he would ever let go of this case, even if Foster asked him to.

~ ~ ~

Chang Chou was frowning as he watched the morning news. Burning the newspaper office to the ground was not near as subtle as he had hoped for when the Tiger had arrived in America. This was a very ham-fisted action that drew far too much scrutiny towards them. It was almost as if the Tiger had wanted to draw attention to his actions. But why?

"Why would he do that?" Chang Chou asked himself. He picked up his encrypted Cell phone and dialed the number he had for The Tiger.

Lǎohǔ had let it ring twice before he had answered. "Hello?" he said in English.

"Where are you?" Chou asked.

"At my Hotel," Lǎohǔ replied.

"Did you torch the newspaper offices?" Chou asked.

"Why do you ask?"

"It was a bad idea. You should have consulted me first."

"I don't answer to you."

"You don't. But you should have at least consulted with me. You have given the Americans a target."

"How?"

"Because they now know for sure that we are watching them."

"Perhaps I have other orders from the Black Dragon Leadership. You are not privy to all that goes on," Lǎohǔ announced.

"This is my operation! Everything is to go through me!" Chou shouted.

"Then perhaps you should call the Dragon's Heart and listen to what they have to say. One must watch the sea to discover the movement of the tides," Lǎohǔ replied softly, and then he hung up, leaving Chang Chou staring at the device in his hand in angry amazement. How dare the Tiger speak so insolently to him? He was a high-ranking member of the Tong, while the Tiger was nothing more than a lowly assassin for hire. And while he hired his services exclusively to the Black Dragon Tong, he had no real standing in the organization.

It appeared that the Tiger had overstepped not only his bounds but as far as Chang Chou was concerned, his usefulness as well. He pulled up the number that would connect him to the secret offices of the Tong back in Hong Kong. He pressed the call button and waited for the call to connect.

Chapter Nine

"Phillips, it's me, Jake. You got any idea where I might find a reporter named Lindsay Call?" Arnold's voice grated in her ear as she tried to wake up enough to answer.

"Why the fuck are you asking me?" Rene Phillips rubbed her eyes, fighting to a wakeful state. She looked over at the clock. It was four o'clock in the morning.

"Do you got any ideas?" Arnold asked again.

"How the hell would I know, Jake? I'm not working on anything about some damned reporter."

"Well, she's involved in some shit about computer chips and the Chinese. I figured maybe you and your new buddies at NCIS might be nosing around in that."

"First I've heard about it, Jake. But I'll ask around and get back to you," Renee Phillips said, meaning it.

"Sure thing, Phillips. Thanks," Arnold replied sounding almost sincere. He broke the connection and she rolled to a sitting position. She was awake now, dammit.

Renee reached for her cell phone and dialed King's number, thinking that there was a good chance that he might have heard something and not shared it. It could well explain why they were looking at Chang Chou and Micro-Com. The more she thought about it the more she liked it. Gut feeling her ass!

"What the hell do you want, Phillips? Do you know what fucking time it is?" Gabriel King's voice filled her ear.

"Yes, I do. It's four o'clock in the morning. What connects Chang Chou, your buddy, with Micro-Com?" she asked.

"Shit! What have you heard?" King asked; his tone curious.

"I just had a call from my former partner asking about a newspaper reporter that he is trying to find that is doing a story on Chinese manufactured computer chips and Micro-Com. I was wondering why he might think I knew something about it."

"It's fucking classified, Phillips."

"Classified? I thought we were partners King? Shouldn't I have been read in on it?"

"It's a need to know, orders straight from the Secretary of the Navy."

"Well, I've got a serious fucking need to know, King. Especially since my ass got woke up in the middle of the fucking night about it."

"I know why now, Phillips. Turn on your television."

"What?"

"Turn on your fucking TV, some of it will become clear real quick," King told her. Phillips walked out to her living room and turned on the television, which was on a local 24-hour news station. The screen filled with a picture of a burning building. A sign identified the structure on fire as the San Diego Recorder.

"Okay, what am I looking at?" she asked.

"I'd say the reason behind the call you got from your former partner," King sighed.

"You think this Lindsay Call worked at the Recorder?"

"I'd say it was a damn good bet."

"What has that got to do with Chinese computer chips and Micro-Com?"

"Who is the largest manufacturer of computers in the United States, Phillips?"

"Micro-Com," Phillips replied, the lights finally starting to come on.

"And where are more computer chips manufactured than anywhere else in the world?"

"China."

"There you go."

"You should have told me."

"I couldn't."

"I'm your goddam partner, King!"

"I had my orders, Renee."

"So did the Nazis at the concentration camps, King. I never figured you to be like them," Phillips snarled.

"I'm not," King sighed.

"Sure couldn't tell it from where I am standing," Phillips told him.

"Would it help if I said I was sorry?"

"Maybe a little."

"I'm Sorry."

"That's beside the point, King. Now fucking apologize."

"I apologize," King said.

"I'll meet you at the office in an hour. You are going to tell me everything about this case then," Phillips told him.

"I'll see you then," King replied before ending the call. Phillips shook her head before setting down the telephone and heading into the bathroom for a shower. Twenty minutes later she was heading for the Naval Yard at Coronado.

~ ~ ~

"So what are your plans for today?" Cooper looked across the table at Lindsay Call. They had finished their breakfast and he had done the dishes and put them in a drainer to dry. They were still sitting at the kitchen table with a cup of coffee in front of them both.

"I've been trying to figure that out," Lindsay told him.

Cooper nodded at that and took a sip of his coffee. "What have you decided?" he asked.

"I want to talk to Jim Carlson at the Department of Homeland Security. He was one person who went on record as being against this deal," Lindsay said.

"Okay, that sounds like a plan. You think he'll give you

an interview?"

"I'm pretty sure. Especially since I have something to trade, like the shit that happened yesterday at the consulate."

"That should definitely get his attention."

"So, what are you going to be doing while I am talking to Carlson?"

"I'm going to take a closer look at Micro-Com," Cooper replied. He had dressed in khaki cargo pants, a white polo shirt and a light blue windbreaker and New Balance walking shoes. His Beretta PX4 Storm was holstered on his hip. He had a digital recorder tucked into a jacket pocket.

"And how pray tell will you do that?" Call looked at him.

"I have my ways," Cooper smiled. They headed for the door and climbed into his truck. Cooper fired up the engine and backed out of the driveway.

~ ~ ~

The Department of Homeland Security was located at 550 W C St #560 on the Naval Base. Cooper got them inside with no trouble. Jim Carlson was actually standing outside and waiting on them when Cooper pulled up to the curb. Carlson opened the door. "You Call?" he asked.

"I am," Lindsay replied stepping out of the truck.

"Who's your driver?"

"Mitch Cooper," he said.

"I've heard of you. She on the up and up?"

"She is. She's got a story to tell. I'll be back in an hour," Cooper told him before Carlson shut the door and watched as he drove off."

"Okay, Miss Call, if you'll follow me?" Carlson told her.

"Lead the way," Lindsay told him.

Cooper swung out of the base and headed for the offices of Micro-Com. He wanted a word with the head man, the one that Lindsay had spoken with the night that she had been shot at. He really didn't plan on taking no for an answer either.

~ ~ ~

Gabriel King looked up as Renee Phillips walked into the squad room. She didn't look particularly happy, but that was something he was used too. Most of his partners were never happy with him. It was something that King had grown used to over the years. It was no big deal to him, but it seemed to be for them.

"Well?" Phillips asked as she stood in front of his desk, fire in her eyes.

"A deep subject for a shallow mind," King smiled at her.

"Dammit King, what the fuck?" Phillips demanded.

"What exactly are you asking?" King looked at her.

"Tell me about whatever the hell was going on at the newspaper and your friend Chang Chou and his friends from China?"

"There is a lady reporter that has been asking a lot of questions. She worked for that newspaper," King shrugged.

"So you think there is a connection?"

"You don't?"

"I haven't made up my mind."

"So what do you think?"

"I think that it is at least a possibility."

"So do I. That's why we are going to go talk to the people at Micro-Com. I want to know exactly what the hell is going on," King shrugged.

"You aren't alone in that. San Diego PD does too."

"You know that you can't tell them anything, right?"

"Yeah, I know that."

"I'm just making sure. You're a good cop, Phillips. I don't want to lose you because of divided loyalties."

"You won't."

"I hope not," King told her.

~ ~ ~

The ride to Micro-Com didn't take long, but King uttered an oath as they pulled into the parking lot. He spotted Mitch Cooper heading for the front doors of the building. "Fuck a duck," King snarled.

"So when exactly did you get into bestiality?" Phillips asked.

"What?"

"You just started talking about having sexual relations with waterfowl and I have to say it makes me uncomfortable," Phillips told him with a straight face.

King grinned at her. "Okay, you got me on that one. Did you see who was just going inside the building?"

"To be honest, no, I wasn't looking."

"Your old pal, Mitch Cooper."

"That is interesting. Why do you think he's here?"

"I don't know, but I am betting we find out."

"I bet we do," Phillips agreed. He parked their car and they climbed out, heading towards the front doors of the corporate building.

"Why the hell is Cooper here?"

"Could he be working with the reporter?" Phillips asked.

"He could. It would certainly explain him being here," King nodded in agreement.

"If Cooper is working with her, then this means that Micro-Com has something to hide. Or he and the reporter think they do," Phillips said.

"Which means that there probably is something going on," King sighed.

"I think that the place is about to get crowded," Phillips said, looking over her shoulder.

"Why is that?"

"My old Partner and his new partner just pulled into the lot as well," Phillips said.

"Well shit," King sighed and rolled his eyes.

"Yep, my thoughts exactly."

~ ~ ~

Mitch Cooper frowned as the elevator climbed up the floors towards the head man's office. Paul Gorman had a lot to answer for as far as Cooper as was concerned. He was pretty sure that somehow Micro-Com was behind the attempts on Lindsay Call's life.

The elevator doors opened and Cooper stepped out into a carpeted hallway and followed the arrows directing him towards Gorman's office. He had questions and he planned on getting answers. It didn't matter if Gorman wanted to answer them or not, he would.

Cooper didn't bother knocking; he just shoved the door open and walked in, given that there was no secretary on duty yet to show him in. Paul Gorman sat behind his desk and looked up as Cooper walked in. "Can I help you?" he asked.

"Probably. The question is will you?" Cooper told him.

"I guess that depends on what you want," Gorman leaned back in his chair as he surveyed the man in front of him.

"You'll talk to me," Cooper told him, giving him a smile that chilled him to the bone.

Chapter Ten

Gabe King and Renee Phillips took the elevator up. They had managed to get going before Jake Arnold and his new partner had reached the lobby, which meant that they would have a limited time with Paul Gorman before Jake Arnold and Santos arrived. Hopefully, Cooper would be willing to share whatever that he might have learned with them.

"How are we going to handle this?" Phillips asked.

"I guess that depends on what Cooper had done before we get there," King shrugged.

"So it does," Phillips agreed. The elevator doors opened and they stepped out into the hall, following the arrows towards Gorman's office. The fact that it was quiet bothered King more than a little. He had expected more. He reached up and gave a quick knock on Gorman's door before pushing it open. The office was empty. So where the hell were Gorman and Cooper?

~ ~ ~

"Onto the roof you son of a bitch!" Cooper told Gorman as he shoved him out into the roof.

"Mister, you are fucking nuts!" Gorman swore as he tumbled onto the roof, ripping the knees of his expensive Armani slacks.

"Why are you trying to kill Lindsay Call?" Cooper asked quietly as he pushed the door shut and wedged it closed with a pipe. He never once took his eyes off Gorman.

"Who the hell is that?" Gorman asked, his eyes finally starting to show fear.

"The lady reporter doing the piece on your microchip deal with the Chinese. She talks to you and somebody takes a shot at her. Last night, somebody burned the newspaper offices to the ground. Only that won't stop the story from getting out. What the fuck is so special about those computer chips?" Cooper asked, his voice never rising and sounding all the more threatening because of it.

"I don't have to tell you a thing, Mister! I'll file charges against you!"

"Oh, you'll tell me," Cooper said as he drew a knife from his pocket and flicked it open with a thumb, stepping closer to Gorman.

"Leave me the hell alone!" Gorman shouted as he crab-walked backward across the roof, trying to get away from Cooper.

"Start talking," Cooper reached down and grabbed a handful of shirt and tie, yanking Gorman to his feet and touching the tip of the knife to his throat, using just enough pressure to start a tiny drop of blood oozing out of Gorman's neck.

"Okay, I'll talk, just please don't cut me!" Gorman pleaded.

"So talk," Cooper said softly. He had learned a long time ago in the Navy that speaking in a soft kind manner while threatening someone was far more frightening than yelling and screaming at them.

"It's the chips. The Chinese have built a backdoor into them that will allow them to take control of any computer that they are built into. They know we have a lot of contracts to build computers for the United States Government," Gorman sighed, twisting his head away from the naked edge of the blade.

"So you're a traitor as well as a crook," Cooper said.

"I guess."

"There is no guessing to it, Gorman. You sold out your country for profit. I should put a bullet in your head right now. But instead, I'm going to turn you over to Military police and I have a digital recording of you admitting to your crime. You can expect them to pick you up within the hour," Cooper told him.

Cooper removed the bar from the door and started down the stairs, leaving Gorman on the rooftop. He hadn't more than stepped out the front doors when Gorman's body hit head first on the sidewalk. Cooper headed for the parking lot and climbed into his truck. Apparently, suicide had been a more acceptable option that a firing squad.

~ ~ ~

"What the hell are you two doing here?" Jake Arnold snarled when he saw King and Phillips walking out of Gorman's office.

"Looking for Mr. Gorman," Phillips replied, frowning at her former partner. "What the hell are you doing here?"

"Investigating an attempted murder," Arnold snapped. He had never liked Phillips and felt that she had betrayed him when she took the liaison position with NCIS.

"Really? We're looking into a possible espionage case," King said.

"You think Gorman's involved?" Arnold glared at the Naval Investigator.

"Yes. Think it might have anything to do with your attempted murder?"

"It might. The reporter was working on an article, something about computer chips when somebody took a shot at her out in front of this place the night before last."

"Sounds like it might tie in. Okay, Sergeant, follow us to the Navy yard and we can exchange information on the case," King said as they all walked to the elevator.

"Cooperation, something I usually don't get from the feds," Arnold noted grudgingly.

"Surprising, given your winning personality," King said as he stepped off the elevator. They looked out through the front windows and noticed a crowd gathering as they shoved out the door.

A dead man lay on the sidewalk, his head a bloody pulp. King looked over at Arnold. "Looks like you might be busy here for awhile."

"Yeah it does," Arnold sighed. He looked over at Santos. "Call it in!"

"On it," Santos replied, jogging towards their car. King and Phillips headed for their ride as well and soon were heading away from the scene.

~ ~ ~

"So, you think that was Gorman that swan dived off the roof?" Phillips asked as they were driving away.

"Yep, I do," King nodded.

"Do you think Cooper tossed him off the roof?"

"No, that's not Cooper's style. He'd have been far more subtle. I think Cooper left the choice up to Gorman and he decided to take the flying leap rather than face the consequences of whatever it was that he had done," King replied.

"So where do we go now?" Phillips asked.

"We find the girl reporter."

"Exactly how do we do that, given that her newspaper burnt to the ground last night?"

"We find Cooper and politely ask him to take us to her," King shrugged.

"Just like that?" Phillips looked at him and rolled her eyes.

"Just like that."

"And how do you plan on finding Cooper?"

"We go see his sea-daddy, Admiral Foster. I'm pretty sure that he will know exactly where we can find Mitch Cooper.

~ ~ ~

Mitch Cooper headed for Coronado and the Office of Naval Intelligence. He wanted to put that recording into the hands of Admiral Foster as soon as possible. He had already downloaded a copy of it into the netbook that he had with him in the truck. He would turn that over to Lindsay when he picked her up. He glanced at his watch. Her hour at Homeland Security was almost up. Dammit, he would need to swing by and pick her up first. He didn't want to take a chance that she might decide to take off on her own and get kidnapped or killed by the Chinese or someone from Micro-Com.

But then again, the Office of Homeland Security was on the base as well, so yeah, he could take care of two birds with one stone. That decided he began making his way through traffic towards the base.

~ ~ ~

Lindsay Call looked across the desk at Special Agent Jim Carlson. He was short and thin with brown hair and blue eyes. He was one of those guys that had the perpetual five o'clock shadow no matter how many times they shaved a day. He was wearing a light gray suit over a white shirt and black tie. His clothes were rumpled like he might well have slept in them the night before. Stray strands of hair curled down onto his forehead, looking like a dark comma.

"As you know, we are not happy about this deal between Micro-Com and the Chinese," Carlson said. A pack of Marlboro cigarettes lay atop his gunmetal gray government-issue desk. Call noticed that there was no ashtray visible and guessed that he probably had to go outside to smoke.

"That's pretty understandable given that Micro-Com does a lot of business with the Government. Do you think that was why the Chinese were so eager to do business with them?" Call asked.

"I think that is a big part of it. As part of our vetting process for the deal, we made Micro-Com give us a random sampling of the chips from random shipments that they had received from the Chinese."

"I'm sure they were not happy about that."

"That would be an understatement. The scary part was what we uncovered when we took the chips apart and studied them, as well as plugging a couple into a pair of computers that were not able to connect with any sort of internet."

Lindsay leaned forward in her chair, her face expectant. "What did you find?"

"There was a code built into the chips. It took us a while to find it. In fact, we didn't until we connected one of the computers to the internet. Then one of our analysts discovered that the chip was transmitting a signal as well as receiving. They were able to isolate it and figure out exactly what it was," Carlson explained.

"And what was it?" Lindsay asked; her eyes wide.

"The computer was sending every bit of information that was in it to another source."

"Another source?"

"China," Carlson said softly.

"So you are telling me that if these chips are in any device, the Chinese could effectively mine data from everyone in the United States?" Lindsay asked.

"Exactly," Carlson admitted.

"So why was the deal allowed to go through?"

"Because the Chinese had some powerful friends over at the State Department, and they had told the President that it would be better for the economy and would help further peaceful and economic relations with the Chinese."

"In other words, it was a political decision."

"Yes, it was."

"I'm sorry but it sounds more like treason to me," Lindsay shook her head.

"Me too, but our hands were tied. That's one of the reasons I agreed to talk to you, Miss Call. I want the

American public to know that they are being sold out," Carlson sighed, leaning back in his chair. He put his hands behind his head and looked up at the ceiling.

"Can I quote you on that?" Lindsay asked.

"You can. I've already put my papers in for retirement and they have been approved. There isn't a helluva lot that they can do to me, Kid."

"Thank you so much for talking to me, Agent Carlson. You don't know how much I appreciate your candor."

"Just make sure the people know." Carlson glanced at his watch. "Cooper should be back by now. I'll walk you out to meet him," he said, standing up.

"Thank you again, Agent Carlson," Lindsay told him as she stood. He opened the door and held it open for her and then walked her back to the front door of the building.

Cooper swung the Chevrolet Sierra 1500 to the curb in front of the Homeland Security building just as the front door opened and Jim Carlson escorted Lindsay Call out. He walked her to the truck and even opened the door for her. "Get the story out," Carlson told her before shutting the truck door.

"I am guessing that things went well?" Cooper asked.

"You could say that. Carlson gave me a bunch of information that I plan on putting in the article," Lindsay said.

"I've picked up some stuff too. Oh, The CEO of Micro-Com jumped off the roof of his building earlier. It's all over the radio," Cooper told her.

"Who knows why traitors kill themselves rather than face justice?"

"Good question. So where are we headed now?" Call asked.

"I have to drop something off at ONI and then I'll let you listen to what Gorman had to say."

"You didn't happen to throw him off of that roof did you?"

"I can say honestly that I did not," Cooper told her.

Chapter Eleven

Admiral Jason Foster was reading through the latest intelligence reports when the knock sounded on his door. He had been expecting it. "Come," he called, raising his voice.

"Admiral," Mitch Cooper said as he pushed his way into the room, accompanied by an attractive brunette.

"What may I do for you, Mitch?" Foster asked.

"I brought you something interesting, Admiral," Cooper told him.

"And the young lady?" Foster eyed him.

"My client," Cooper replied. He slid the digital recorder across the desk to Foster. Foster looked down at it.

"What is this?"

"Proof that Paul Gorman of Micro-Com was in full collusion with the Chinese to commit treason against the United States," Cooper shrugged.

"Interesting," Foster noted.

"What do you want me to do with it?" Foster looked across at his former agent.

"I'd think that you would want to use it to reveal that Micro-Com was about to commit treason against the United States," Lindsay said.

"But isn't that your job, Miss Call?" Foster fastened his cold blue eyes on her.

"It is. But it is also your job to investigate charges of treason," Lindsay replied.

"That is certainly true," Foster nodded.

"So what are you going to do?"

"I will have my agents investigate," Foster told her.

"Let's get out of here Cooper, this guy is a joke," Lindsay

frowned. Cooper glared at Foster and couldn't help but agree. Then he thought about it and realized that Foster planned on playing a longer game than that. He wanted to get not only Micro-Com but the people from the Chinese side as well.

Cooper gave the Admiral a surreptitious nod before following Lindsay out and caught the Admiral's wink. He closed the door. "That was a big fucking waste of time!" Call snarled as they headed for the front door.

"Maybe not," Cooper told her as they stepped outside into the open.

"How can you say that?" Call glared at him.

"Right now, you are just looking at the short term goal, exposing this deal for what it is. I think Admiral Foster is looking for a long-term solution that will keep anything like this from happening again," Cooper explained as they walked to his truck.

"How?" Call asked her voice much calmer after taking a moment to consider his words.

"He wants to embarrass the Chinese by letting them know how easily their attempt to get the information they shouldn't have was to spot. So easy that a mere girl reporter was able to spot it. To do that, he needs to draw them out."

"In other words, he's hanging us out as bait."

"That's one way of looking at it. But honestly, Lindsay weren't you putting yourself out there as bait anyway to try and force the Chinese to make a move so that you could get your story?" Cooper asked her.

"I guess I was. That's why my boss hired you. To keep me safe while I did that," Call nodded.

"It is. Now the newspaper has been burned to the ground. So it seems like your boss was right to hire me."

"Yes it does," Call nodded.

"So, who do you want to talk to next?"

"I need to think about that. I need to write up what you

got from Gorman and e-mail it to my boss along with a quote or two from your pal the Admiral."

"Lindsay," Cooper looked at her.

"I promise not to crucify him. Yet," she smiled evilly. Cooper rolled his eyes and shook his head. He hoped Admiral Foster would understand that he had put himself in the crosshairs and there was nothing Cooper could do about it.

~ ~ ~

Gabriel King swung his car into a parking spot in front of the Office of Naval Intelligence on the Coronado Naval Base. Phillips eyed him expectantly from the passenger seat. "Well?" she asked.

"Now we go in and beard the Admiral in his den," King said, throwing open his door and stepping outside. Phillips rolled her eyes as she followed his lead and joined him as he headed for the front door of the building. His NCIS ID and her San Diego PD ID got them in the door and an escort to the Admiral's office.

King gave Phillips a warning look as they approached the Admiral's door. He wanted her to pretty much remain in the background during the interview. Phillips was okay with that. She wanted a chance to observe King's interaction with a superior officer. She felt it would be interesting. Would King defer to his rank? Or would he go for the throat? She was curious.

The escort knocked on the door and a voice called for them to enter. The escort went in first to announce them. Phillips thought it was strange. King seemed to take it in stride. Phillips took in a deep breath and let it out slowly.

"Gabriel, how are you?" Admiral Foster stood, extending his hand. King took it and shook it, and then he settled into a chair across the desk. Phillips took the second seat.

"I'm doing well, Sir. Do you know where I might find

Mitch Cooper by any chance?" King asked.

"How would I know, Gabe, Cooper is no longer in the Navy."

"You were his Sea daddy."

"That was a long time ago, Son."

"Cooper and a woman he is protecting are persons of interest in my investigation," King said.

"What investigation is that?" Foster leaned back in his chair and made a pyramid with his hands. He looked at King expectantly.

"Chang Chou is in San Diego. We both know that he and Cooper were adversaries. We both know why."

"So why the interest in Cooper?" Foster asked.

"He's working for a reporter that has uncovered a story with National Security implications."

"So what does that have to do with me?" Foster gazed at him without blinking.

"I think you know a lot more than you are telling me."

"Do you?"

"I do."

"So again why are you here?"

"I'm here because I'm trying to find answers," King said.

"I don't have any for you," Foster told him.

"I wish I could believe that, Admiral."

"Believe what you want, King. I don't know where Cooper is right now," Foster smiled. King didn't like it, but he knew he was telling the truth.

"Admiral, would you say that you and Mitch Cooper are close?" Phillips asked suddenly. Foster turned his attention to her, focusing on her face.

"We are," Foster said after a few seconds.

"Then you should know that because of this case, the Chinese will be sending people to kill him. Shouldn't you be at least a little concerned about that?"

"To be honest, Miss, I'm more concerned for the agents they send after him. Mitch Cooper was not only one of the most effective intelligence agents I ever had under my command but one of the most highly decorated SEAL commanders. I can tell you for a fact that Mitch Cooper won't go down easy. If the Chinese send people after him, they do it at their own risk," Foster told her.

"I see. Thank you for your time, Admiral," Phillips said before turning and walking out of the office with King on her heels. He waited until they were outside of the building before speaking.

"What the hell was that all about?" King demanded.

"I just wanted to make sure that the Admiral knew what the stakes were," Phillips replied.

"Phillips, he knew what the stakes were before we ever walked in there. He's purposely distancing himself from Cooper right now to avoid any fall out if this thing goes south," King told her.

"Does Cooper know that?"

"It was probably Cooper's idea. But there is one thing," King said, pausing.

"What's that?" Phillips asked.

"I have a feeling that the Admiral is hiding something about this case. And I'm not sure that even Cooper knows about it."

"Then I suggest we find Cooper and make sure that he knows it. You think he might visit that McP's bar? I understand it is something of a SEAL hangout."

"He might at that. At the very least, if we leave a message there for him to contact us, it will get to him. So I guess that's our next stop."

"Then let's get moving," Phillips told him. King nodded and they headed for the car.

~ ~ ~

Jake Arnold and Luke Santos sat in the squad room.

They had been at Micro-Com the better part of the day. The apparent suicide of Gorman had been messy on several different levels. The positive thing that had come out of it was that it had allowed Homeland Security to come and put a halt to the deal between Micro-Com and the Chinese. At this point, Arnold was ready to call anything positive a win in this case. He still wanted to talk to Call but it appeared that she had dropped totally off the grid. That bothered him.

Jake didn't like things that bothered him. It kept him up at night, and he was a man that liked his sleep. He looked across the desks at Luke Santos. "We need to talk to the editor at the newspaper that burned down last night," Arnold said.

"Why is that?" Santos asked.

"Doesn't it strike you as a little odd; that the newspaper that the reporter works for suddenly burns down, she disappears, and Gorman jumps off a building? I mean, come on," Arnold rolled his eyes.

"You think he'll know where Call might be?"

"It's worth a shot," Arnold shrugged.

"I'll see if I can find a home address for him."

"Do that," Arnold sighed.

~ ~ ~

Chang Chou was furious. His position had been usurped by the Tiger. This was supposed to be *his* operation. It appeared that there was unrest within the Black Dragon Tong and that he might well be sacrificed in the power struggle that seemed to be going on.

Lǎohǔ was part of the power struggle, though Chang Chou was not sure which of the triad that led the Tong that Lǎohǔ worked for. It was enough that the Tiger had his own agenda and Chang Chou had no idea what it was. That was most disheartening and unacceptable for him. Was it the reporter? Or the man who seemed to be protecting her? He needed to know if he were to take this operation back under his own control. He had to determine that at all cost!

~ ~ ~

Cooper lifted his hands. He saw the man sitting behind the desk. The man who seemed to be in charge folded his hands and gazed back at him. "You made sure that your men made it out of the warehouse, even though it meant that you would be captured," the man said.

"I have no idea what you are talking about," Cooper said.

"You know, American. And you will eventually tell me everything you know."

"I came on my own. I don't like you guys."

"In the words of your countrymen, bullshit. You will tell me what I want to know."

"I wouldn't bet on that," Cooper smiled, his eyes bleak.

~ ~ ~

"Cooper, are you okay?" Lindsay Call asked.

"Yeah, I am," Cooper shot her a glance and hoped that she didn't know that he was lying. He wasn't okay and it all led back to China and that mission to recover those computer chips. He felt like he was in the fucking twilight zone, where the past and the present were overlapping. He took a deep breath and let it out slowly.

"You don't look like you're okay," Call told him.

"I suppose not," Cooper said.

"But you expect me to believe you?

"That is up to you. What I expect you to believe is that I am doing the best I can to protect you," Cooper told her.

"I do believe that," she said. "But I can also tell that something is bothering you. Service related stuff?

"Yeah, service stuff. Bad memories from bad times."

Chapter Twelve

Lǎohǔ sighed. Chang Chou was acting childish and it was causing irreparable harm to the actual mission that he had been sent to the United States to accomplish. So far, he had not managed to find his target. He had been told that burning the newspaper would flush his true target out into the light, but so far, that had not been the case. That meant he might have to resort to far more drastic measures.

The Tiger had an address for the female reporter. Perhaps if he searched there he might find some clue to his real target, the man that had given him the scar that bisected his left cheek. The Navy SEAL that had almost killed him, making his escape from the factory in Hong Kong.

Lǎohǔ frowned at the memory. This was a personal thing, but it was also in the best interest of the Tong. The Black Dragon Tong were about to become major players on the international stage, and only the death of the American could make that happen.

The Navy SEALs prided themselves on keeping their identities secret, hiding behind code names. But Lǎohǔ had learned the name of the man that had given him the scar so long ago. The man had seemed proud to tell him who it was that had marked him forever. Mitchell Cooper. Now, Cooper was going to die for his impertinence!

~ ~ ~

"Let's head over to the Navy Yard at Coronado. I want to find out what that fucker King knows," Jake Arnold said as he stood up from behind his desk.

"We may as well. We've pretty much wrapped up the Gorman suicide," Luke Santos agreed.

89

"I still ain't convinced the guy jumped," Arnold growled.

"Why is that?" Santos asked.

"Because Mitch Cooper has a hand in this mess," Arnold replied.

"How do you know that?" Santos was curious.

"Because I can smell that son of a bitch!"

"You have a real problem with that private eye, don't you? Is it because of your former partner?"

"Maybe. Mainly it's because I don't like the fucking asshole!"

"I can buy that," Santos nodded with a grin.

~ ~ ~

Phillips and King were back in the NCIS offices. Phillips looked across her desk at King. "So why are we here?"

"We're here because your former partner expects to find us here," King replied.

"You know this how?" Phillips asked him.

"Because I told him we would meet him here, so this is where he will look for us," King said.

"You don't think he'll be tied up still with the Gorman case?"

"Nope. He'll by now have decided that somehow Mitch Cooper is involved in it."

"You seem sure of that."

"He hates Cooper."

"Yes, he does. He blames Cooper for you taking this position as liaison with NCIS. Despite what you might think, Arnold liked having you for a partner."

"I don't buy that for a minute."

"It's true. He resents me and he hated Cooper with a passion."

"Then why is he coming here?"

"Because he wants to find a link between Cooper and Gorman's death."

"And he thinks you will help him do that?"

"He does."

"But you won't?"

"No. Because while I dislike Cooper too, he is damn good at what he does. If anyone can expose this crap that the Chinese are trying to pull, it is him."

"But you have your own beef with Cooper."

"I do, but I can live with it. I'm not sure that Jake Arnold can," King told her.

"So what do we do?" Phillips asked.

"We stall Arnold so Cooper can do whatever it is he is trying to do," King replied.

"I hope that this doesn't blow up in our face."

"Me too."

~ ~ ~

Jake Arnold and Luke Santos had to sign in at the door before they were admitted to the elevator that would take them to the offices where NCIS was located. Arnold's cigar had gone out and he chewed on the stub, fidgeting as the elevator took them upwards. It was the first time he had ever been in the place. He hadn't been sure what to expect, but it looked like pretty much their own squad room at the police station, other than the big wide-screen television monitors where they could blow up images from their computers. Arnold wasn't a fan of computers either, for that matter He preferred typing out his reports on an old Smith Corona Selectric typewriter downtown. Santos was suitably impressed, though.

"This is pretty state of the art," he said with a low whistle.

"Just a bunch of electronic voodoo," Arnold waved his hand dismissively.

"Still..." Santos let the thought die as Gabriel King stood and waved them over to his desk.

"Detectives," he said by way of greeting, before sitting

down again.

"I found out that Cooper had been at Micro-Com. What's his involvement in this mess?" Arnold asked pointedly, his cigar dangling from the corner of his mouth.

"This is the first we have heard of him being involved," King regarded the San Diego cop coolly.

"I doubt that very much," Arnold removed the cigar and stabbed it towards King.

"You need to remember, Detective; that you are here at my invitation. I can just as easily have you removed from the base," King said, his voice icy cold.

"Listen, there is no reason why we can't work together on this thing," Luke Santos cut in, trying to smooth what he assumed was a case of ruffled feathers.

"Maybe," King never took his eyes off Arnold as he spoke.

"We know that Cooper is involved, and it seems to be because of the reporter that got shot at. We just want to know if he was involved with Gorman's death," Santos said.

"If we see him we'll ask him. Have you considered that maybe the Chinese killed Gorman? Or that he committed suicide because he got caught with his hand in the cookie jar?" Phillips asked, inserting herself into the conversation that she had been silently watching.

"No, we hadn't," Arnold glared at her.

"Maybe you should," Phillips met his gaze unblinkingly.

"You always were sweet on the son of a bitch."

"Fuck you, Jake. You always were an asshole and for your information, I fucking hated working with you," Phillips told her former partner.

"Fuck you, Phillips. You always acted like you were so much better than me, but you never were!" Arnold snarled.

"Well if you two are finished with your verbal orgy, I suggest you two leave and leave now!" King's voice cracked like a whip.

"You gonna make me, Big Man?" Arnold spun around to face him.

"If I have to," King stood.

"No need for that. Security, please escort these two men off the base," Deputy Director Kenneth Danvers said to the four beefy guards that suddenly appeared in the squad room.

"This isn't over, King," Arnold snarled at him.

"It is as far as I'm concerned," King replied.

"Special Agent King, you and Detective Phillips need to come to my office right now," Danvers ordered.

"Yes, Sir," King replied but he was making it sound like cur. Phillips shook her head as she followed the Deputy Director towards the stairs. King followed slowly.

~ ~ ~

"Cooper, there is more going on than what you're telling me. What is it?" Lindsay Call asked. Cooper was driving them to a different safe house. He had gone to his place and put the truck in the garage. They were now in his red Mitsubishi Eclipse.

"It was an old mission, one back in my SEAL days. We were sent into Hong Kong to raid a manufacturing plant and warehouse for some computer chips that were being developed by the Chinese. I think that they are the same ones that you are doing your story about," Cooper told her.

"Wow. How long ago was that?" Call looked over at him.

"Ten years," Cooper told her.

"Seems like a long time ago. Seems like this has been in the works a long time."

"It has. There was a man in charge. They called him the Tiger. He was smarter than we thought and had set a trap for my team. I got my men out, but I was captured," Cooper said.

"Oh wow."

"Lǎohǔ was his name. I'm not sure if he worked for the

communists or one of the tongs. He tortured me, trying to get me to confess that I was there as a spy. I never did."

"My God, Cooper. How did you escape?" Call asked.

"My Team came back for me and got me out. It wasn't long after that that I transferred to Intelligence work," Cooper told her.

"And the man named Lǎohǔ?" Call asked.

"He disappeared. Until now," Cooper told her.

"You know this for sure?"

"He was the one that burned down your newspaper office. It fits his M.O.," Cooper replied.

"Wow. You are sure of this?"

"I am."

"Cooper what the hell are we going to do?" Lindsay demanded.

"I'm going to protect you and we are going to make sure your story gets published to embarrass the Chinese," Cooper told her.

"I like that plan, but can you keep us alive if the Chinese are trying to kill us to keep it from getting out? I mean they did burn down the newspaper I work for," Call shook her head.

"You let me worry about keeping us alive. Now, who do you want to talk to next?"

Call looked at him for a moment, then dug a notebook out of her bag and flipped it open. "Calvin Petrie, U.S. Trade Administration. They have an office here in San Diego."

"That makes sense, given that San Diego is a major port in the United States."

"You know how to get there?"

"I do," Cooper grinned in reply. His dark sunglasses masked his eyes. Knowing that the Tiger was out there stalking him had him on edge. He still had nightmares about that warehouse in Hong Kong. He wasn't going to tell Call that however. No, that was something that he would keep to himself or talk to Dr. Crane about. Not that Dr. Crane had been that much help, but the shrink was a good listener and he had top secret clearance.

They didn't talk anymore as Cooper guided the red sports car through the streets of San Diego. Cooper had the radio dialed to Jazz 88.3, San Diego's premier Jazz station. They were doing a tribute to Chet Baker.

Mellow sax sounds filled the car. Cooper was glad for the silence. It allowed him to think as he drove. He needed to draw Lǎohǔ out into the open and still protect Lindsay. The question was how to do that. He would let her talk to Petrie on her own and while she was talking to him, he would enlist a little help from his friends. Cooper nodded top himself, happy with his plan.

~ ~ ~

Calvin Petrie was more than happy to talk to Lindsay about the Micro-Com deal. It was obvious that he was no happier about it than the guy at Homeland Security. He ushered her into his office and offered her a seat across his desk from his own. He secretary entered and waited. "Would you like some coffee or water?" Petrie asked her.

"Coffee would be nice," Lindsay smiled back at him, playing to him. Lindsay wasn't above using her womanly charms to help get information. Petrie looked at his secretary. "Two coffee's please."

"Yes, Sir," she replied, turning and disappearing out the door. Petrie settled his gaze on her.

"Now, Miss Call, how may I help you?" he asked.

~ ~ ~

Cooper dialed a number from his contact list and listened to the ringing as he waited for it to connect. "Hello?" asked a voice on the other end.

"I could use some help, Smoke," Cooper said.

"Mitch? Is that you?" Samuel 'Smoke' Kowalski asked.

"It's me, Smoke. I need some help. Do you know how to

get a hold of Boom and Flipper?"

"Of course. Hey, I heard you were working as a Private eye and security consultant these days."

"You heard right Smoke. Right now I'm working on a case that connects to our Hong Kong mission."

"How soon do you need us?"

"As quick as you can get here. Call me when you get in," Cooper said before he broke the connection. Smoke, Boom, and Flipper were former teammates. Ones that had survived Hong Kong. He knew they would come, and he knew that he would need them.

Chapter Thirteen

"Thank for your time, Mr. Petrie. I really appreciate it," Lindsay Call told the rep from the U.S. Trade Administration.

"It was my pleasure, Miss Call. I hope when your story breaks, it will put an end to this travesty," Petrie told her.

"Me too, Mr. Petrie," Lindsay said as she turned and walked out of his office. Petrie had given her a lot of information not only about Micro-Com but also about the Chinese company that was manufacturing the chips. She had enough to go public with it! She wondered if her boss was still her boss since the offices had burned to the ground. She pulled out her cell phone and dialed George Rain's number.

"Call, where the hell have you been?" Rain demanded.

"Doing my job. I've been working the story, Boss."

"E-mail it to me when you get it written and I'll make sure it gets out. Is Cooper with you?"

"He's been sticking like glue," Lindsay replied.

"Good. Do what he says and follow his lead, Call. I have to tell you, this story scares the hell out of me," Rain told her.

"It does me too," Lindsay said.

"Then you are finally getting smart, Call."

"Gee thanks, Chief," Lindsay rolled her eyes, hanging up. Cooper picked that moment to roll up in front of her.

"Done here?" he asked. Call climbed into the Eclipse.

"Yes, and what I got was pretty good stuff. Can you take me somewhere where I can write it?"

"Sure thing. Another safe house. Given that we have the Chinese looking for us, I want us to stay on the move as much as possible."

"Sounds like a pretty good idea. You really think they would kill to keep this story from getting out?"

"They burned down your newspaper didn't they?"

"Yeah, they did," Call admitted quietly. Cooper put the car in drive and glided smoothly back onto the street, blending into traffic.

Smoke Danvers dialed the telephone, punching in a Key West number. "Boom-Boom Salvage," announced a gravelly voice on the other end of the call.

"Boom, it's Smoke. Is Flipper hanging out with you?"

"Of course, we partnered up in this marine salvage operation. Why?" Boom asked.

"The Captain needs us out in San Diego. Said it's related to Hong Kong," Smoke told him.

"We'll head west on the first available flight," Boom told him.

"See you in San Diego," Smoke said before breaking the connection. He had his own packing to do. But he could carry armament since he'd be flying his own plane. Hong Kong. Wow. That was a clusterfuck from the word go. He shook his head at the memory.

~ ~ ~

Smoke cursed as the lights came on! It was a fucking trap! Coop started firing at the Chinese soldiers that were popping out of hiding.

"Get out!" Coop yelled covering his team. The Chinese started shooting as well and bullets were whizzing through the air all around them. Smoke fired off a long burst from his MP-5 and headed for the window that they had come through. Flipper and Boom went out ahead of him. Moses was right behind him and didn't even have time to scream as his head exploded from a bullet going through it. Smoke spun around once he was out the door, providing cover fire

for Coop and Sticks. A grenade went off and Sticks went flying through the air, coming apart before landing. Cooper hit the floor and the fire from the Chinese was too intense. There was no way Smoke could go back in, so he and Boom and Flipper got the hell gone from the area. They would regroup and plan a rescue later. Right now, it was too damn hot to stay around...

~ ~ ~

Lǎohǔ frowned as he looked at his cellular phone. It was Hong Kong. He answered it. "Yes?" he said in Chinese.

"Is your mission complete yet?" asked a voice on the other end.

"Which one? Stopping the reporter or eliminating the target?" Lǎohǔ asked.

"Both. Chang Chou has been complaining."

"I will deal with Chang Chou in my own time. The newspaper threat has been eliminated. The SEAL is another matter."

"Wrap it up soon, Lǎohǔ. We cannot allow these threats to linger."

"I understand," Lǎohǔ replied before breaking the connection. Chang Chou was becoming a problem that would have to be dealt with soon. He was not a part of the mission, but he thought that he was running it. Lǎohǔ would have to demonstrate to him that he was not.

~ ~ ~

Cooper took Call to a safe house he maintained in Chula Vista. It was one of several he maintained in the city in case of trouble. A trick he had picked up during his days working for the ONI. It was one that had proven useful in his work as a private investigator.

Cooper escorted her in and set about making them something to eat as she settled at the kitchen table with her computer and notes and started writing her story. He wanted to ask her a number of questions about what she had found out but figured she would be more likely to let him read it after it was written. He thawed some hamburger in the microwave and broke it up in a skillet to brown. He rummaged a box of Velveeta Nachos helper from the pantry and opened it. Once the hamburger was browned, Cooper added water and the sauce mix, and then the pasta.

Cooking actually relaxed him, though he would never admit it to anyone that actually knew him. He liked changing up recipes to give them extra flavors. It was part of what he enjoyed about cooking.

~ ~ ~

Lindsay Call was intent on her writing. She noticed Cooper in the doorway but ignored him as she worked. She didn't have time for conversation at the moment and she sensed that Cooper knew that as he disappeared back into the kitchen.

~ ~ ~

Cooper found a bag of Fritos corn chips and a tub of sour cream. He had the salsa from the box to add once the pasta was soft. He wondered how long it would take for Smoke, Boom, and Flipper to arrive. It would be good to see them all again. It had been too long. Eddie had come back to his team after Hong Kong, but that didn't matter now. Eddie was dead too.

Cooper shook his head. Now wasn't the time to think about Eddie or Hong Kong. He turned on the small television that he kept in the kitchen, switched it over to an all-news channel. Cooper lifted the lid off the skillet and stirred the mixture inside. The water wasn't boiling yet, then put the lid back on and walked back to the counter with the television.

The apparent suicide of Paul Gorman was the lead story. His co-workers at the executive level were baffled as to why he had done it. After all, hadn't he just inked a major deal with the Chinese that would make the company tons of money. Cooper shook his head, baffled at the corporate greed. Gorman had jumped because Cooper was going to out him for treason. He had a feeling that several other bigwigs at Micro-Com would go down as well.

Foster's plan was to let Call's story out them and then swoop in with federal agents and scoop them all up. Cooper didn't care much for that plan because it put Lindsay in danger. And despite himself, Cooper was starting to like her.

Sure, she was abrasive and irritating and full of snarkiness and sarcasm, but she was also pretty doggone cute. He shook his head, trying to clear it. Sure it had been a while since Kara had left, but he was pretty sure it wasn't just lust. Still, it was something that he needed to be careful about. Caring too much. It would just get them both into trouble. Trouble of a kind that he just didn't need on his plate with The Tiger on his back trail.

"That smells really good," Lindsay said as she walked into the kitchen.

"It will taste even better when it's done," Cooper flashed her a smile with even white teeth.

"I'll take your word for that. Have you got anything to drink here? And I mean real alcohol, not just beer," Call said.

"I think I can find something," Cooper told her, walking over to the fridge. He opened the door and pulled out a bottle of Canadian Mist. "Will whiskey do?"

"Hell yes. Pour me two fingers straight, no ice. Nobody civilized dilutes their whiskey with ice."

"As you wish," Cooper said over his shoulder as he got two six-ounce tumblers down. Cooper uncapped the whiskey and poured two fingers into each before recapping the bottle and carrying both glasses over and handing Lindsay one. "You send your story in?" he asked.

"I did. According to George, it will go up on the website

by morning."

"Then this is a celebratory drink then?"

"Pretty sure it is," she smiled.

"Good."

"You're not so bad, Cooper," Lindsay sipped at her drink.

"Thanks, I think," Cooper told her.

"Don't sound so surprised. You know I kind of like you too. How about after we eat, we go upstairs to the bedroom?"

"Are you sure that's what you want?"

"It is. I like you, Cooper. I don't meet many men that I want to sleep with. You're one of the lucky ones," Call told him.

"Gee whiz, I don't know what to say," Cooper grinned again.

"Say yes, and then feed me. I'm starving," Call grinned back.

Cooper headed back to the stove and stirred the mixture in the skillet. He turned the heat down to a simmer. "Food will be ready in about ten minutes," he told her.

"Good," Call said as she pulled his face down to hers and kissed him.

~ ~ ~

Lǎohǔ looked at the address that came across his cell phone. He put the car in drive and headed that direction. The GPS was a good guide. It would lead him to Cooper and then he could settle with the former Navy SEAL once and for all.

Lǎohǔ rubbed his face with his hand as he drove. He looked at his right hand. It shook. Part of it was from adrenaline he was sure. Some of it might be anticipation that after all these years he would finally get his revenge.

Mitch Cooper was the only prisoner that had ever escaped from him. That was a blot on his record, not only with the government but with the Tong as well. It was something that Lǎohǔ could allow to go unaddressed. No, he needed to kill Mitch Cooper to secure his own reputation as an unstoppable assassin.

~ ~ ~

George Rain read the story that Call had sent. It named names and gave attributable sources. He smiled. Call had done a good job. He started editing the story and making sure it was fit to be published on the World Wide Web. They may not have a print office for the moment, but the San Diego Reporter was still a viable newspaper!

Cooper was turning out to be well worth the money that Rain had invested in him. That was a good thing. He smiled. Call didn't seem to like the guy, but he was doing the job that he had been paid for.

~ ~ ~

Cooper pulled Call close to him as their lips met. He opened his mouth and felt her tongue probing into it. He pushed her against the wall kissing her back just as hard as they explored each other's mouth with the kiss. Cooper pulled up her blouse and slid his hands underneath it. He found her breasts and squeezed them through her bra. His hands moved around behind her and unhooked the bra. She pulled her blouse over her head and tossed it to the floor.

Cooper slipped her bra off of her and cupped her breasts in his hands, his thumbs rubbing her nipples, making them hard. He could feel her hands undoing his belt and then his pants. He felt them sliding down his thighs. He hooked his thumbs in her panties and worked them down her legs. Cooper kissed the thatch of hair there.

His tongue leaped out and slipped into the folds of flesh between her legs. He heard her gasp with pleasure. Cooper dived in deeper, tasting her as he probed deeper with his tongue. Call groaned with pleasure, digging her fingers into his hair.

Chapter Fourteen

Smoke had texted Cooper when he landed, and Cooper had texted him back an address. Smoke had rented a jeep and had his gear in a duffle in the back. Boom and Flipper were a couple of hours behind him, but they would be along soon enough. Right now the most important thing was getting to Cooper. Especially, if as Cooper thought, the Tiger was out there looking for him. Coop wasn't one to ask for help, so Smoke knew that the shit had to be ready to hit the fan. Hong Kong had been a nightmare for all of them. A couple of the guys had paid the ultimate price and it still killed Smoke to this day that they hadn't been able to bring Stick's body back. He had left a teammate behind once, but he had vowed it would never happen again.

Using the GPS in the rental car, he drove through the streets of San Diego. The house he was going to was not the one listed for Mitch Cooper in the city directory or on Google. It figured that his old boss would have safe houses set up around the city. Standard Operating Procedure for SEALs and spies. Mitch Cooper had been both. Smoke pulled into the driveway, looking around. Nothing stood out to him. He grabbed his duffle and walked to the front door and rang the bell. It took a few seconds but then Cooper opened the door. "Thanks for coming," he said, waving Smoke inside. Cooper was wearing a gray V-neck tee shirt and a pair of Olive drab cargo pants. He had a pistol shoved into his waistband.

"So, what is going on?" Smoke asked, closing the door behind him.

"Lǎohǔ is in town. He torched my client's newspaper to make a point," Cooper shrugged.

"Sounds like that asshole."

"It does."

"So what are we going to do about it?" Smoke asked.

"We are going to take the Tiger down," Cooper told him.

~ ~ ~

Lǎohǔ checked the submachine gun on the seat beside him. It had taken a great deal of effort, but he had finally managed to track down where Cooper was holed up. He had a type 85 submachine gun on the seat beside him and a Beretta F-92 pistol holstered beneath his left arm. He guided his rental car down the street. Soon Mitch Cooper would discover that the past could come back to kill him. The past never dies, it only postpones the inevitable.

Lindsay pulled on sweats before climbing out of the bed. It had been a while and Cooper had managed to really rock her world. She hoped that he understood it was a heat of the moment kind of thing and that she wasn't looking for anything long term. It had more to do with a reaffirmation of life than anything else.

It also helped lay to rest the tension between them, something that she was grateful for. She liked Cooper, sure. But she also understood that they had been through some pretty harrowing shit together and that sometimes that could make a moment seem like more than what it was. What had happened earlier with Cooper was a moment, nothing more. Still, it was a moment that she wouldn't mind repeating.

She heard a second voice from downstairs as she pulled a tee shirt over her head. She didn't bother with a bra before heading down to see who their visitor was. Cooper was talking to a dark tall man with dark hair and a highly developed upper body, much like Cooper's. "Who's your friend?" Lindsay asked.

"This is Smoke, one of my former teammates from my

SEAL days," Cooper said by way of introduction.

"And this is?" Smoke looked at Lindsay and she could see the lust in his eyes. She smiled.

"Lindsay Call, newspaper reporter and my client. She's working on a story that will expose a Chinese plan to infiltrate the United States computer networks with computer chips that give them a secret back door into all of our systems," Cooper explained.

"Wow," Smoke whistled appreciatively.

"Our old pal, Lǎohǔ doesn't want the story coming out."

"I can see why he wouldn't."

"Not to mention, it would cost him and the Black Dragon Tong a whole lot of money.

"I want to know more about this Black Dragon Tong," Lindsay told them both.

"You are better off not knowing," Cooper told her.

"He's right," Smoke added.

"Hey, if they are sending a guy to burn down my paper and probably kill me, then I think I ought to be in the loop," Call told them both. Smoke looked at Cooper.

"She does have a point," Smoke said.

"Yeah, and I hate it when she's right, Cooper sighed. Call rolled her eyes and stuck her tongue out at Cooper, drawing a smile from Smoke.

"She doesn't make it easy, does she?"

"Not one bit."

"You both realize I'm right here in the room with you, right? Stop talking about me in the third person."

"See what I mean?" Cooper grinned. Both men started laughing.

~ ~ ~

"You brats were playing me just then," Call said, it suddenly dawning on her,

"We were," Smoke chuckled.

"Maybe a little," Cooper grinned. Call felt a tiny shiver

run through her stomach at the sight of that grin.

"So about the Black Dragon Tong?" Call pushed her earlier thought down and focused her attention on the two men.

"Let's go to the kitchen," Cooper said, turning and leading the way. He grabbed them each a bottled water from the fridge and sat the water down on the table, so they could all take one. He unscrewed the cap from his and took a long pull before sitting it on the tabletop before speaking.

"The Black Dragon Tong originated in Honk Kong back in the early nineteen hundreds. It was started by a Triad made up of Kim Lun Soon, Chang Ki Sek, and Chak King Lo. They were three businessmen who came together to form what started out as a secret society to fight government oppression. But as their influence grew, they realized that they needed money to influence the government. So they expanded into criminal enterprises.

"As they began to realize monstrous profits, the triad realized that they enjoyed the power that wealth gave them. They began actively recruiting street level soldiers and drawing other businessmen into their secret society. Eventually, they formed the Black Dragon Tong and set themselves up as part of the secret overlords of Hong Kong.

"Their influence grew and spread across China and other countries in the Pacific Rim, like Vietnam and Japan, North and South Korea. They even spread to the United States in a limited fashion, usually setting up in various big city 'Chinatowns'. Their influence spread into legitimate business and corporations. They actually own the company that is manufacturing the computer chips," Cooper explained.

"Oh my God. You're saying that this is less of a government thing than a criminal enterprise slash terrorist attack?" Call looked at him, her eyes wide.

"It is all three because the Tong has infiltrated the

Chinese government as well," Smoke told her.

"That's a lot to take in," Lindsay said, taking a large drink of her water.

"It is," Cooper agreed.

"This would make a good sidebar article to the one about the computer chips."

"I'm sure it would. Except for every bit of it is considered classified material," Cooper told her.

"In other words, I can't use a word of it."

"Not unless you want to spend time in a Federal Prison," Cooper told her.

"Dammit, Cooper!" Call started. He cut her off.

"You wanted to know about the Black Dragon Tong. Their top hitman, a guy called The Tiger is in San Diego and he is hunting for both of us. So I called in some help." Cooper told her.

"Your buddy here."

"And a couple of others that will be here soon. These guys were part of my team when we were all Navy SEALs."

"You think four will be enough?"

"I hope so," Cooper said honestly.

~ ~ ~

San Diego International Airport.

Boom and Flipper scooped up their checked bags and headed for the rental car office to get a vehicle. "At least our guns didn't raise any alarms," Flipper said.

"That's why I insisted on the Glocks," Boom told him.

"I gathered that."

"Have you called Smoke or Coop yet?"

"Nope, I figured that was more in your prevue, being the senior guy."

"I'm only a month older than you."

"And I bow to your senior wisdom oh ancient one," Flipper grinned.

"When this is over, if we survive it, I'm going to kick

your ass all around the block," Boom told him.

"Sure you will," Flipper grinned.

~ ~ ~

"So why aren't we out hunting for this Chinese assassin?" Phillips asked. King looked at her for a long moment.

"Because he's going to make himself known soon enough. Burning down the newspaper office was just a feint to draw our attention in a direction away from his real target." King told her.

"His real target? Do you know who that might be?" Phillips demanded.

"Sure. It's Mitch Cooper," King shrugged.

"You plan on letting him kill Cooper?"

"Cooper can take care of himself. In fact, if anyone can beat the Tiger, it's Cooper. He managed to escape from the Tiger back in the nineties when he was a Navy SEAL," King told her.

"Why am I just now finding out about this?" Phillips demanded.

"I dunno. Maybe because you never asked."

"You are almost as bad as working with Jake Arnold."

"Hey, no need to be insulting," King frowned at her.

"I said almost."

"You did."

"So do we try to find Cooper and warn him?"

"He already knows. No, we are going to go annoy Chang Chou and see what we can get him to spill," King shrugged.

"You think that will work?" Phillips asked.

"We won't know until we try."

"I'm getting a headache."

"Should I stop so you can get some Midol?"

"Fuck you, King!" Phillips snarled.

"No thanks, Phillips, we work together." King grinned at her.

~ ~ ~

Lǎohǔ guided his car to the curb. He could see the house that he had traced Mitch Cooper to half a block away. He reached over and picked up the Chinese type 89 submachine gun from the seat beside him. He stepped out of the car and pulled back the charging handle as he walked down the sidewalk.

The afternoon sun dappled the sidewalk beneath his feet as he walked, beams of sunlight burning down to glare off the cement sidewalk beneath his feet. He lifted his face for a moment, letting the sunlight warm it. Then he looked at the house and started down the sidewalk towards it. He lifted the submachine gun to his shoulder and his finger was tightening on the trigger when the front window exploded outwards under a hail of bullets.

Bullets ripped the air around him and forced The Tiger to the ground before he could return fire. His finger curled around the trigger and the submachine gun began spraying lead into the house. The garage door lifted and more gunfire came from that direction, forcing him to race to the corner of the house to seek cover.

A red car shot out of the garage in reverse, swinging around in the street and then burning rubber as it shot away. Lǎohǔ stepped out from the corner of the house and fired, but he knew that he had missed. Mitch Cooper had managed to escape him once again! Lǎohǔ ran to his car, but by the time that he had managed to turn it around and head after the red car, it was long gone. He slammed his fist on the steering wheel in frustration and then drove back to his hotel.

Chapter Fifteen

"That was way too close," Smoke said as Cooper drove them away from the safe house.

"It was. I'm trying to figure out how he tracked me to an off the books safe house purchased under an assumed name," Cooper replied.

"Because the Chinese are goddamned efficient. Don't sell them short," Smoke told him.

"I never have," Cooper replied.

"So what do we do now?" Lindsay Call asked from the back seat.

"We find a new place to lay low."

"That sounds like a good plan."

"I thought so," Cooper told her, not taking his eyes off the road in front of him. About that time, smoke's cell phone rang. He pulled it out and looked at it. "It's Boom, he and Flipper have arrived."

"Answer it and have them meet us at McP's," Cooper told him.

"Roger that," Smoke said before relaying instructions via cell phone.

"Can you keep me alive, Cooper?" Call asked from the back seat.

"I'll do the best I can," Cooper told her.

"That is not all that reassuring," Lindsay sighed.

~ ~ ~

McP's Irish Pub is owned by former Navy SEAL Greg McPartlin and is located on Orange Avenue in Coronado. It is a place where both active duty and former SEALs like to congregate and swap stories of past and present adventures of derring-do. Leann Mertz was behind the bar when

Cooper, Storm, and Lindsay Call walked in. She waved at Cooper and sent a waitress over to the table that they had selected, one near the back that put a solid wall at their backs. Cooper and Storm positioned themselves where they could see the front door and cover the entrance from the back as well.

"Two Killian's Red and a Fireball for the lady," Cooper told the waitress. She nodded and headed for the bar.

"Looks like we beat them here," Smoke said as his eyes scanned the crowd. The jukebox was playing something by *Flogging Molly*, but Smoke didn't recognize it.

"There are a few familiar faces," Cooper pointed out.

"God, Mitch, are some of these guys even old enough to drink?" Smoke shook his head.

"We used to be that young once, my friend."

"Not that I can remember," Smoke shook his head.

"Good to see you, Mitch," Leann appeared next to them with the drinks. She looked at Cooper's companions for a long moment. "Smoke? My God it is you!" she exclaimed.

"I figured that maybe you had forgotten me by now, Leann," Smoke grinned up at her.

"Not bloody likely, Smoke! Greg is going to be sorry he missed you guys. He's up in L.A. looking to expand," Leann told them.

"Greg was always looking to make a fast buck, Cooper chuckled. Leann sat their drinks on the table eyeing Call.

"And who is the lady?"

"My client. The Chinese are looking for us. Boom and Flipper should be getting here soon. Can you make sure they find us?" Cooper asked.

"I can do that," Leann told him.

"Thanks, Leann," Cooper told her.

Lǎohǔ paced in his room. Cooper had eluded him once more. Where would he go next? Lǎohǔ knew that he had to anticipate Cooper's movements if he were to have any chance of eliminating both him and the female reporter. It seemed that she was becoming more of a problem than he had been led to believe. The San Diego Police were looking closely at Micro-Com after Gorman had jumped off the roof. The burning of the newspaper office had drawn far more attention than he had been led to believe it would. Chang Chou appeared to be trying to divert blame from himself onto Lǎohǔ. That was something that he, Lǎohǔ, would not tolerate. No, it was time to remove Chang Chou from the equation and replace him with someone more competent.

Lǎohǔ pulled an encrypted cell phone from his pocket and dialed an international number in Hong Kong. He began to speak in Mandarin when a voice answered on the other end. The conversation lasted for approximately twenty minutes. Finally, Lǎohǔ ended it and disconnected the call. He smiled, but it never came near his eyes.

Lǎohǔ dialed another number, a local one and began asking questions. The Black Dragon Tong had eyes everywhere. Once he put out the word, he knew that it would not take long for him to get an answer.

~ ~ ~

Boom and Flipper walked into McP's. The crowd was loud and raucous and pretty normal. The Jukebox was playing an old Beach Boys tune, *California Girls*. Both grinned at the memories that the song evoked as their eyes scanned the customers. They spotted Coop, Smoke, and a pretty brunette. The two men made their way to the table. Coop and Smoke stood and embraced them both with a lot of backslapping.

"So what the hell is going on?" Flipper asked. Flipper was lean and mean with long blond hair and blue eyes. He looked like a runner with extra wide shoulders.

"The Tiger is in town," Cooper told him, Flipper froze.

"The head guy from that factory?" he asked, his eyes

wide.

"The very one," Cooper replied.

"I understand why you called," Boom replied. He was a fireplug of a man with wide shoulders, thick arms, brown eyes, and short brown hair.

"Why is the Tiger here?" Flipper asked. Flipper was actually Phillip Harrington the third. He was a deep-water demolitions specialist.

"My client uncovered something that the Chinese government doesn't want to get out," Cooper explained.

"Which is?" Boom asked. Boom was actually one Bob Oscar Morris, again a demolitions specialist and underwater salvage diver.

"That factory that we raided that was making those funny computer chips? Turns out they have a code built in that will allow them to take over any computer that they are embedded in. They got the contract to build chips for Micro-Com which has a contract with the department of defense," Cooper explained.

"Oh, Shit!" Boom said quietly.

"That pretty much sums it up," Cooper nodded.

"So what do you need us to do?" Flipper asked.

"I need you guys to keep the Tiger off of me and Lindsay until I can help her get her article published and blow the deal."

"That's all?"

"Yes."

"Piece of cake, Cooper," Boom grinned in a lop-sided fashion.

"I told you they'd go for it," Smoke grinned too.

"Coop, dealing with The Tiger is some serious shit," Flipper said softly. Flipper looked like a California surfer dude but was a specialist in weapons and tactics. He was also a karate master.

"This whole business is serious shit, Flip. Admiral

Foster is backstopping us as much as he can, but he needs for us to get the job done through civilian means, which is Ms. Call here. She already had most of the story uncovered before I signed on," Cooper explained.

"Under the table and off the books, standard ONI protocol," Flipper shook his head.

"Hey, if it's that big a deal, you don't have to stay. You can get right on back to Florida and I'll pay for your ticket."

"Fuck you, Coop. You called and I came, that means I'm in for the long haul. You don't back out on your team."

"I appreciate that Flip. I know this brings back a lot of bad memories for all of us."

"Hong Kong will always be a place filled with bad memories."

"It will. Here comes the waitress, what are you boys drinking?"

"Killian's red of course," they both chimed in at once. Cooper ordered theirs and another for him and Smoke as well, plus two more shots of fireball for Call.

"So what's the plan?" Boom asked.

"That is what we need to figure out," Cooper told him.

~ ~ ~

Sid Galecki looked around the office he had inherited from Paul Gorman. Sid was short and wide, with a belly that strained the buttons on his shirt. A blue tie hung at half-mast. His hair was slicked back and salt and pepper gray and black. Thick dark eyebrows stood out over his eyes. He had been Gorman's second in command so when the boss jumped off the roof that put him in the hot seat.

Galecki sighed as he began pulling open the drawers of Gorman's desk. Gorman had kept him in the dark about the details of the deal with the Chinese. Now he needed to know what those details were. The board was asking questions and Sid needed to be able to answer them, especially with all the publicity that Lindsay Call was stirring up with her story about the deal. He hadn't read it yet, but it was still making him sick to his stomach as he worried about what it might say. Fucking Gorman had fucked them all over by killing himself.

~ ~ ~

"This what you expected?" Phillips looked over at King as they approached the shot up house.

"I actually expected to find some dead bodies," King replied.

"Are you disappointed that you didn't?"

"Given the reputation of this Chinese guy? Hell yes."

"I guess this mean's Cooper was better than you gave him credit for," Phillips smiled thinly.

"I guess so. Except judging from the brass, there were at least two guns firing back," King told her.

"You think Cooper had help?"

"I don't think that the reporter was shooting back."

"Probably not."

"Then Cooper had help."

"Any idea who it might have been?"

"Not a fucking clue," King told her. Right about then, Jake Arnold and his new partner pulled up. Phillips rolled her eyes and walked back inside the house. She would let King deal with Arnold.

Phillips wandered around inside the house. It was obvious that Cooper had set it up as a safe house. For who? The reporter? Likely. Cooper realized that he had to hide her. The big question was who had found the place and how? The Chinese were likely suspects.

Phillips walked up the stairs to the second floor. There were two bedrooms up there. From the looks of it, only one had been used. She shook her head. It surprised her to think that Cooper might be sleeping with his client. He didn't seem like the type. But then again, Call was an attractive woman, so she couldn't really blame him.

She liked Cooper, and she was fairly certain that he liked her too. But there had never been anything romantic between them. Currently, she was happy about that. Or she thought she was. Phillips shook the thought away as roamed the house.

~ ~ ~

"Why the fuck are you here, King?" Arnold asked.

"I'm pretty sure that Cooper was using this place as a safe house, protecting that newspaper reporter from Chinese assassins," King replied.

"Goddamn it! Chinese fucking assassins in San Diego?" Arnold glared at him.

"I didn't exactly invite them," King said, showing his empty hands.

"Yeah, I figured that," Arnold growled.

"I know you did."

"I don't like these fuckers shooting up my town."

"Believe me, Detective, I don't either."

"I suppose not, King. Where the fuck is Cooper?"

"I wish I knew," King said.

~ ~ ~

"I got an idea," Boom said.

"So let's hear it," Cooper told him.

"We use her as bait. The Tiger will come after her. When he does, we take him down," Boom shrugged.

"Just like that?" Cooper looked at him.

"Just like that."

"What if the Tiger is smarter than that?" Cooper looked at him.

"You think he is?" Boom asked.

"He could be."

"Then I guess we are fucked."

"We're fucked and Lindsay is dead."

"You like her, don't you?" Boom asked.

"I do. She's got a set of brass balls."

"So we keep her alive," Boom shrugged.

Chapter Sixteen

Chang Chou was furious! He kept his expression impassive but his almond-shaped eyes blazed with anger. He was incensed to learn that Lǎohǔ was attempting to stage a coup within the Black Dragon Tong. The Tong was divided and at war within itself. That could only lead to its destruction!

Chang Chou had worked very hard to rise to his current position in the Tong hierarchy. It was not a position that he was willing to give up. Lǎohǔ was on some sort of vendetta, rather than coming to help him with the reporter problem. That meant that Lǎohǔ had to be stopped before he ruined everything!

Control of the world would be determined *if* the deal was sealed with Micro-Com. Because if the chips could be implanted inside the computers used by the Americans Department Of Defense computers, the Chinese government could take over them at will. Then China would become the greatest superpower on Earth.

Chang Chou picked up his phone and dialed his most trusted lieutenant. When Ping Song picked up, Chou gave him his instructions in Chinese. Ping Song acknowledged his orders and hung up. For the first time in several days, Chang Chou smiled.

~ ~ ~

Cooper led the others to another safe house and parked his red Eclipse in the garage, switching this time to a white panel van with no windows in the back. It had plenty of room for his friends and their equipment, as well as providing Lindsay Call with a mobile workstation.

They had taken time out to eat as well. "So what now?" Call asked him.

"Have you got enough to publish your story?" Cooper asked her.

"Almost. I still need to talk to Aaron Becklund at the Defense Logistics Agency. They are one of the agencies that oversees buying things like computer chips for the U.S. government," Call replied.

"Call him and get an appointment. While you are talking to him, we are going to start beating the bushes for Lǎohǔ. I'm tired of reacting and I want to go on the offensive for a change," Cooper told her.

"Sounds good."

"I'm going to leave Smoke with you as a body guard until I can pick you up again."

"Okay."

"He'll protect you every bit as well as I can. But I need to get on the hunt for the Tiger and see what I can do about evening up the odds," Cooper told her.

"So let's do this," she said as she pulled out her telephone and dialed the number for Becklund from memory. Cooper was amazed at how well prepared she was for her end of the hunt.

~ ~ ~

Lǎohǔ had stopped to eat at a small Chinese restaurant. The food was passable but lacking in the authenticity of real Chinese food. It was very obvious that the real owner was anything but Chinese. He ate the tasteless food and left a mediocre tip before exiting the restaurant and heading back out on the streets.

The sun was starting to go down, and the air was cooling rapidly. A breeze wafted in from the ocean, carrying a tinge of salt in the air. Somewhere in the city, he would find Cooper and Lindsay Call and he would kill them both. That was preordained. When he returned to China, it would be as a victor, and he would then assume leadership of the Tong.

"I think it is time we actually talked to Chang Chou," King said, driving towards the hotel where the Chinese agent was staying.

"That sounds like a good idea to me too," Phillips said. King looked over at her, surprised.

"Why is that?" he asked.

"Because Chang Chou has been involved in this from the word go. I think he probably brokered the deal with Micro-Com for the chips," Phillips shrugged.

"I think so too," King agreed

"So what are we going to do?" Phillips looked at him as he drove.

"We talk to him and let him know we have enough to put him away and see what he is willing to trade for it," King replied.

"That actually sounds like a good plan."

"I do come up with them occasionally."

"So I see."

~ ~ ~

Lin Chow spotted the rental car that Lǎohǔ had been said to be driving and swung his own ride to the curb. He pulled out his mobile phone and dialed the number for Chang Chou. "I have him," he said.

"Where are you?" Chou asked.

"Outside a restaurant."

"I am sending you reinforcements."

"Okay, but I won't need them. He doesn't suspect a thing."

"Don't get too cocky. Lǎohǔ is not called the Tiger for nothing."

"I know that."

"Wait for your back-up. I don't want him to know that we are hunting for him."

"Sure thing, Boss," Chow broke the connection, never

taking his eyes off of his target. Not even when a young woman bumped into him.

"Sorry about that," she said, giving him a smile that would melt the heart of the sphinx.

"No problem," Lin Chow said, never taking his eyes from his target. He felt hard metal jab into his side.

"I can't let you kill The Tiger. My Boss wants him too."

"I have no idea what you are talking about," Chow replied.

"Sure you don't," Phillips told him.

"Please leave me alone, young lady."

"You are under arrest, Mr. Chow." For the first time, he moved his eyes to look at her. She was petite with blonde hair, a pretty face and she was smiling at him, showing dimples on each of her cheeks. However, the Glock pistol pressing into his side showed that she was entirely serious.

"Go ahead and put your hands behind your back said a male voice from directly behind him. Chow let out a long sigh as his shoulders slumped and he moved his arms behind him. A hand roughly grabbed his right wrist and he felt the first touch of the metal cuffs before spinning to his right, his left leg sweeping the woman's legs and dropping her to the sidewalk, her gun clattering out of her hand.

He whipped his right wrist free of the man's grip and shot his left fist at the man's face. The older man blocked the fist and spun the opposite direction and sent a spinning back kick into Chow's side, driving him backward.

Lin Chow launched himself forward in a flying drop kick, but the other man dodged and spun driving his left fist into Chow's face. The Chinese agent hit the sidewalk and the man pounced on him, driving his face into the concrete. Chow felt his nose break and twin gouts of blood sprayed onto the sidewalk. He felt handcuffs fasten tightly on his wrists and then he was being hauled roughly to his feet.

"Time for you to go to jail," the woman told him as she

re-holstered her Glock. Chow looked over at the man.

"Who are you?" Chow asked.

"Gabriel King, NCIS. Now get in the car," King snapped back.

Chow frowned, glancing over his shoulder at the building where his target waited. There would be others that could be sent.

~ ~ ~

Lǎohǔ had spotted the disturbance across the street. So, it appeared that the war within the Black Dragon Tong had begun. He did not know who his two American benefactors were, nor did he care. It was enough to know that they appeared to want him alive.

As long as he was alive, he had a very good chance of accomplishing his mission and killing Mitch Cooper once and for all. First, Chang Chou must be dealt with. Lǎohǔ paid for his meal and slipped out the back entrance, knowing that it would be some time before his watchers realized that he was gone.

"How did you know this guy was hunting Lǎohǔ?" Phillips asked as King sent them hurtling towards the Naval Base at Coronado.

"Because he's one of Chang Chou's top lieutenants. I have the faces pretty well memorized of everybody that works for Chang Chou," King shrugged.

"But now this Lǎohǔ is in the wind and gunning for Cooper."

"Cooper can take care of himself, believe me. We're going to park this guy at Coronado and then head for Chang Chou's hotel and pray that we aren't too late."

"I'd feel a whole lot better about this if we could get a hold of Cooper and let him know about the shitstorm headed his way."

"Cooper already knows, and if I know Cooper even half as well as I think I do, he's already brought in some help.

Don't worry about Cooper."

"How can you be so sure?" Phillips asked.

"Because I know Cooper," King shrugged. Phillips shook her head, not sure if she would ever understand King or Cooper. They were clearly of a breed that she hadn't even known had existed.

~ ~ ~

"I have a hit on the Tiger," Flipper announced from the rear of the van.

"When and where?" Cooper asked.

"Chinese restaurant near Coronado ten minutes ago."

"He's already moved. Check for a guy named Chang Chou," Cooper directed.

"Who the hell is he?" Flipper asked.

"Chang Chou is the top man for the Black Dragon Tong in the western United States. He is most likely the man that called Lǎohǔ in. So he's also the most likely to know where the Tiger can be found."

"That makes sense."

"It does."

"Okay, searching now," Flipper replied.

~ ~ ~

Smoke glanced around the office of Aaron Becklund of the Defense Logistics Agency. It had the sparse furnishings of most government offices, utilitarian gray paint on the walls to match the battleship gray metal desks that were situated in the bland maze of cubicles filling the space.

Becklund himself was a typical government drone, round and balding, pale watery eyes behind thick-lensed glasses, a white shirt, and brown tie and pants, a brown jacket hanging off the back of his chair. His hands were thick and his fingers slab-sided. He regarded Lindsay Call with interest as she sat down across from him. Smoke remained standing and leaned against the wall outside the cubicle's entrance where he could see them both. Call seemed perfectly at ease as she pulled out a digital recorder and turned it on before placing it on the desk between herself and Becklund.

"As you know, Mr. Becklund, I am here inquiring about the upcoming trade deal between Micro-Com and the Chinese manufacturing giant Hieu Electronics. I am given to understand that Homeland Security and your offices have gone on record as opposing this contract," Lindsay said.

"You would be correct. The Chinese are insisting that they be allowed to embed proprietary software in the chips that they sell to United States companies. Those of us in the purchasing and logistics feel that this would be unethical and even dangerous. If we buy chips with unknown codes written on them, it could very well undermine our own national security," Becklund told her.

"So you are saying that these microchips would be very dangerous to National Security?"

"They would. We don't know what these embedded codes might allow the Chinese to do with these chips if they are placed in any electronic device here in the United States."

"That is pretty scary."

"Yes, it is. However, Paul Gorman over at Micro-Com has been putting a lot of pressure on us to seal this deal."

"Paul Gorman committed suicide earlier today. Haven't you heard?"

"I hadn't but that means that there is a chance that we might be able to stop this from happening. I thank you for that new information, Miss Call," Becklund smiled at her with yellowed teeth.

"My pleasure, Mr. Becklund," Lindsay smiled back.

~ ~ ~

Cooper pulled into the parking lot of Chang Chou's hotel. Flipper had found the registration info. "How you want to play this, Coop?" Boom asked from the rear of the van.

"I'm thinking we play it by ear. What's the SEAL motto?" Cooper asked.

"Adapt and overcome," Boom replied.

"Which is exactly what we are going to do. Boom, you're on me. Flipper, you stay here to provide whatever kind of support we might need."

"You think you're going to need support?" Flip asked.

"I'm counting on it," Cooper replied as he shut off the engine and opened the door of the van. Boom was already out of the passenger door. The two men were already moving towards the motel as the van doors swung shut. Flipper just shook his head.

Chapter Seventeen

Flipper watched as Boom and Cooper headed for the hotel entrance. Support? How the hell was he supposed to support them from out here? What the hell was Cooper thinking that he would be able to do from the outside? He shook his head and dragged his duffle bag from the rear to the front of the van. The stuff had been brought along by Smoke, *'just in case,'* his old teammate had said. Flipper zipped the bag open and looked inside whistling. Smoke would have made one hell of a boy scout!

Flipper pulled out a MAC-10 chambered in .45 caliber and four magazines. He slapped one into the magazine well and put the other three on the passenger seat. He added a Browning Hi-Power in 9mm to his waistband. He pulled out two smoke grenades. He didn't know if they would be useful but they would help confuse the Tiger or any other Tong soldiers that showed up. Flipper sat back in the driver's seat smiling and feeling a whole lot more comfortable.

~ ~ ~

Cooper and Boom stepped inside and headed for the desk. Boom distracted the concierge while Cooper stole a look at the registrations ledger that lay open on the desk and got Chang Chou's room number. He nudged Boom as he stepped past him and in a few seconds Boom joined him at the elevator doors.

"You get it?" Boom asked.

"I got it," Cooper replied.

"So let's do this." The elevator doors opened and they stepped inside. Cooper punched the number button for the floor that they wanted, and then for the next two floors above it. That would help provide a confusion factor if things went south.

~ ~ ~

King swung his car into the hotel parking lot. Phillips was acting as nervous as a long-tailed cat in a room full of rocking chairs. He knew that she liked Cooper. Liked Cooper a whole lot more than she liked him. That was evident. It didn't bother Gabriel King, though. He was all about catching the bad guys. If Cooper was the bait, so much the better. While he and Cooper had made their peace with the death of Cooper's protégé, there was no love lost between them. Cooper was merely the means to an end.

King didn't see any of Cooper's vehicles that he recognized so maybe they had beat him here. He hoped so. Chang Chou would be able to help them bag the Tiger. That would be a big feather in NCIS's cap if it happened. Plus it would shut down a major Chinese spy ring operating in the United States.

"Cool it, Phillips, otherwise you'll give us away before we even get close," King told her.

"I'm cool," Philips replied, wishing that she believed it. She had no fucking idea what King had in mind.

King swung his car into a parking place and shut off the engine. He looked over at Phillips. "Renee, I need to know if you are with me on this."

She took a long moment before replying. "I am. I hate that Cooper might walk in and get caught in the crossfire," Phillips said.

"Cooper knew the risks when he took the job."

"Did he know that the Tiger was after him?"

"Maybe not at first, but I can guarantee that he knows by now and is ready for him."

"You better fucking be right about that, King. Otherwise, I may fucking well shoot you myself!"

~ ~ ~

Lǎohǔ drove slowly towards Chang Chou's hotel. He

had contacted men that he could trust and they were converging there as well. It was time for Chang Chou to die. He had spent too much time interfering in Lǎohǔ's plans.

His cellular phone rang and he answered it. One of his agents reported that Mitch Cooper and another man had entered Chang Chou's Hotel. Lǎohǔ frowned as his foot pressed more heavily on the accelerator.

The car accelerated. He needed to get to Chang Chou before Cooper did. Cooper could not be allowed to speak with Chang Chou!

~ ~ ~

Chang Chou paced back and forth in his room. He had hoped to hear from Lin Chow by now. Apparently, he had failed in his mission. That meant that Lǎohǔ was out there and was coming for him. He spoke in Mandarin to his bodyguards and they took up defensive postures inside the suite of rooms. Chang Chou walked back to the bedroom and dialed the number of another one of his lieutenants. Kung Pow answered.

"Lǎohǔ is attempting a coup within the Black Dragon Tong. We cannot allow him to succeed. I want all of our people on the streets and he is to be shot on sight," Chou ordered.

"As you command," Pow agreed, breaking the connection.

Chang Chou smiled. His men were loyal, and they were very, very good at what they did. He did not believe that Lǎohǔ could best them.

~ ~ ~

Cooper was the first man out of the elevator and was moving down the hallway at a fast clip. There was one man standing in front of Chang Chou's door. He gave Cooper little attention and paid even less to Boom who had followed Cooper out of the elevator. Cooper waited until he was right beside the bodyguard before he made his move.

Cooper slammed a fist right into the man's throat, causing him to gag and grab for his Adam's apple. While he was busy choking on his own blood, Cooper drove his elbow into the man's temple and put his lights out for good.

"Nice moves, Coop. Good to see you haven't lost a step," Boom told him appreciatively.

"Not a one," Cooper replied as he turned the doorknob and stepped inside. Cooper had his Beretta Storm PX-4 in his hand as he moved deeper into the hotel suite. Boom had drawn his .44 desert eagle as well. It could drop a rampaging rhinoceros at fifty yards. More than enough to handle Chang Chou or the Tiger. If he was able to get a shot off.

~ ~ ~

Chang Chou spun around as the door to his suite flew open. He had almost expected to see Lǎohǔ standing there. Instead, it was two Americans. One blond, the other dark. Both held guns in their fists. "Chang Chou, we need to talk," the blond said, smiling disarmingly.

"Who are you and why are you here?" Chang Chou asked, unflinchingly.

"I'm the guy protecting the reporter looking into your computer chip deal with Micro-Com, the one you've been trying to kill."

"What reporter? What deal? I am a lowly businessman working for my government."

"Maybe, but isn't your first allegiance to the Black Dragon Tong?"

"The who? I know nothing of the Tongs."

"Bullshit, Pal. But what the hell, maybe we'll leave and let The Tiger have you," the blond said.

"Lǎohǔ is coming here?" Fear showed on Chang Chou's face.

"Yes, he is. So unless you want us to leave you to him, you need to talk to us."

"I will talk," Chang Chou hung his head. If the Tiger was coming he was as good as dead anyway. Not even these two men with guns would be able to protect him.

"Talk to me about the micro-ship deal," the blond said.

~ ~ ~

Lăohŭ pulled into the parking lot and parked his rental car. He stepped out into the cooler evening air. The sun had set and night was rapidly falling. Lăohŭ smiled. Darkness was his friend. Though he was Chinese, he had trained in the Japanese art of ninjitsu. In his homeland, he was often referred to as a Ghost walker. The Ghost Walkers were the Chinese equivalent of Ninjas. One time he had served an ancient warlord called Chi Pei. But Chi Pei had died, leaving him on his own.

Lăohŭ had drifted aimlessly until he found a home with the Black Dragon Tong. Then, and only then, he had found a purpose for his life. But over the past few years, the Tong had suffered from dissent within, fracturing into factions. It was Lăohŭ's dream to unite those factions once more. If he could do that, then he would fulfill his dreams and The Black Dragon Tong would rule the world!

Lăohŭ moved through the shadows like a ghost. His dark clothing blended with the dark. Every sense was alert as he entered the building through a side door. He avoided the lobby as he made his way to the elevators. He took one to Chang Chou's floor. Stepping out of the elevator, he saw a man crumpled to the floor in front of Chang Chou's room.

That could only mean that Mitch Cooper was inside. Lăohŭ smiled. That meant he could kill two birds with one stone as the saying went.

He headed down the hallway. The Tiger smiled as he stalked down the corridor. At last, he would have his vengeance on the one man that had ever escaped from him.

~ ~ ~

"I helped develop the computer chips. You Americans

disrupted our first attempt to flood the market with them by bombing our factory in Hong Kong. But we kept working until we found a company that was willing to look the other way over some of our proprietary software installed on the chips," Chang Chou explained.

"Micro-Com," the Blond supplied.

"Yes."

"So why now?"

"We saw an opportunity and we took it," Chang Chou shrugged.

"I believe you," the blond said. "Now you need to get the hell out of my country and never come back. This deal is over and off the table forever. If you try it again, I will find you and I will blow your fucking head off," the blond told him.

"I agree," Chang Chou nodded his acceptance of the deal.

"Good," the blond told him.

The door flew open a second time. Lǎohǔ filled the entrance. The dark man fired at him and the Tiger avoided the bullet as he moved into the room. The blond fired and scored a hit that caused the Tiger to stumble. The dark man fired again as Lǎohǔ dived out of the room. The two men charged into the corridor, leaving Chang Chou behind them.

~ ~ ~

Lǎohǔ winced in pain as he ran, hitting the door to the stairwell and caroming down the stairs. He had not expected there to be two men with Chang Chou. They had caught him unaware and he had paid a price for it.

The pain was not as bad as it could have been and for that he was thankful. But it was bad enough. He ran. It was the first time since Hong Kong that he had ever failed. Mitch Cooper was bad luck for him. He needed to change that.

~ ~ ~

Cooper had charged out into the hallway and saw the stairwell door close. He started for the door and shot a look over his shoulder at Boom. "Take the elevator down to the ground floor!" he yelled. Boom nodded and headed for the elevator.

Cooper ran to the stairwell and threw the door open, his Beretta leading the way. He started down the steps, listening for any sounds that the Tiger might make during his descent.

~ ~ ~

Flipper looked up as he heard the distant sounds of gunfire. From the sound of things, Cooper had lured his target in. Flipper watched the hotel, his eyes scanning for anything unusual. He clutched the MAC-10 in his fists.

He wanted a chance to take The Tiger out. Flipper stepped out of the van and started moving forward towards the hotel. The side door bursting open caught him by surprise and as he swung towards it, flame blossomed from the weapon in the man's hands. Flipper felt something strike him and drive him backward. He hit the ground with a groan as warm wetness spread across his chest. He was dying and he knew it. The Tiger had managed to kill him after all this time...

~ ~ ~

Cooper ran out into the parking lot. A car was screeching out of the lot onto the street. He saw Flipper and ran to him, dropping to his knees beside his old friend and swim buddy.

"Fuck!" Cooper screamed into the night.

Boom moved up beside him. "Shit happens, Pal. Flipper knew that when he signed on." Boom told him.

"I know that. It doesn't help," Cooper said.

"Not at the moment. But in the future."

Chapter Eighteen

King and Phillips could smell cordite in the air as they stepped off the elevator. Both of them drew their guns and held them at the ready as they headed towards the room that belonged to Chang Chou. The door was open. King started swearing under his breath as he swung into the doorway, his pistol extended in front of him in a proper shooter's stance.

A man was huddled next to the windows, bullet holes surrounded by spider webs of cracked glass. King moved deeper into the room, every sense on high alert. He could feel Phillips moving right behind him, watching his back. The man huddled on the floor raised his head and blinked at them both.

"Are you hurt?" King asked.

"The bullets missed," Chang Chou said in heavily accented English.

"Did your pet Tiger try to turn on you, Chang?" King asked, keeping his pistol on the Chinese agent.

"So it appears," Chou sighed. "May I stand?"

"Please do, but keep your hands where I can see them."

"As you wish Agent King. I find myself at your mercy," Chou said.

"Better mine than The Tiger's," King shrugged, holstering his weapon. "You want to talk about it?"

"I don't see how I have any choice."

"What will your pals in the Black Dragon Tong have to say about that?"

"The Tong is devouring itself from within. Soon it will be no more," Chou shrugged.

"You sound sure of that."

"The Tiger tried to murder me. If not for the intervention of two of your countrymen, he would have succeeded."

"Turn around and put your hands behind your back, Chou. We need to make your arrest official."

"As you wish, Special Agent King," Chou said as he complied. Phillips kept her gun aimed at the Chinese agent until King had him cuffed, then she holstered her weapon and they escorted Chang Chou out into the corridor and headed for the elevators.

"That seemed a little too easy," Phillips said.

"Sometimes it works that way," King replied.

~ ~ ~

Cooper and Boom had taken the van and slipped away from the hotel parking lot. Using a burner phone, Cooper called the police and reported the shooting of his former teammate. He hated leaving Flipper back there. The SEALs had a motto. No man left behind. For the first time in his life, he felt that he had broken his oath. Because they had left Flipper behind. Sure he was dead, but that didn't make it right.

"It's okay, Coop. You called the cops. Flipper will be taken care of and it will be done right," Boom said from the passenger seat.

"Flipper is dead and it's my fault. I should never have called you guys in," Cooper shook his head.

"Bullshit, Coop. Flipper agreed to come. He knew that this could happen when we answered Smoke's call. We all knew that it could happen if we were going up against The Tiger. We all knew what he was capable of after Hong Kong. You more than anybody. You want to make it right, then we take the Tiger down once and for fucking all!" Boom said savagely.

"We'll get that bastard for good," Cooper said softly. He had needed to hear Boom out. For a few minutes there, he had been feeling sorry for himself. Sorry for the loss of his friend. But now, that had been replaced by a cold rage. A slow burning fire that would only be quenched by the death of The Tiger!

~ ~ ~

"Who the fuck is this guy?" Jake Arnold asked as he climbed out of the car.

"Don't know yet," Luke Santos replied. "But I'll talk to the first responders."

"Do that," Arnold said, chewing on the stub of a thick cigar protruding from his lips. He looked around the parking lot. No sign of cameras. Shit! That would make it harder to figure out what the hell had gone down here. Arnold frowned. This had the smell of Mitch Cooper all over it, just like the dead guy at Micro-Com, but there was no evidence to link Cooper to it.

Arnold wasn't totally sure that Phillips and her new NCIS partner weren't jerking his chain over Micro-Com. He didn't like Special Agent King any more than he did Cooper. Both of them were fucking assholes as far as he was concerned.

The whole Chinese angle to the case bothered him as well. It had spook shit written all over it. Cooper had been a spook before turning private eye. He had been able to find that much out the last time. He spat out the stub of his cigar and pulled out another, stripping off the cellophane wrapper and tucking it into the corner of his mouth. Arnold pulled out a lighter and fired it up. He exhaled a cloud of blue smoke into the evening air.

Luke was walking towards him. "What have you got?" Arnold asked.

"There were a couple of people in the parking lot when it happened. They saw an Oriental guy running across the parking lot. This guy climbed out of a van and the Oriental guy shot him. A couple of minutes later, two men came out of the hotel, checked the body, then climbed into the van and drove off," Santos reported.

"Did they say what the two guys looked like?" Arnold asked.

"Just that one was blond and the other had dark hair."

"Put out an all-points bulletin for Mitch Cooper. His smell is all over this," Arnold snarled.

"You sure you want to do that?" Luke asked him.

"Yeah, I'm sure. Mitch Cooper is involved in this shit to his fucking eyeballs. I want to take that motherfucker down once and for all."

~ ~ ~

Lǎohǔ blinked his eyes as he drove. He needed to find a safe place to go to ground and soon. He recognized the signs. He was going into shock from the bullet wound that he had sustained in Chang Chou's room. He headed for San Diego's version of Chinatown. There he would find a place to have the bullet removed and start healing. Mitch Cooper was proving much harder to kill than he had anticipated.

The American agent had the luck of the devil himself. Lǎohǔ forced his eyes open. His side was wet. He was bleeding badly. He needed medical attention and he needed it quickly. Otherwise, Cooper and his friends had won.

Lǎohǔ parked the car and stumbled out onto the street. He had an address to look for and fortunately it was not far from where he had parked. Lǎohǔ made his way to the door and knocked loudly. After several heartbeats, the door opened and he was ushered inside.

"You are hurt, Lǎohǔ," the old man said that ushered him inside.

"I have been shot. I need your assistance," Lǎohǔ replied.

"Of course. Did the American do this? I told you seeking vengeance was foolish."

"Perhaps you are correct, Little Father. But for my

honor, it is something I must do."

"You put far too much emphasis on honor, my son. You should look to the future, not the past. The past is dead."

"No, Little Father, the past never dies! It is with us always. It is with me anyway. I lost face when the American spy escaped! The only way to regain my honor is to kill him!"

"And if you fail?"

"Then I will die trying."

"If you are going to be that foolish, my son, why should I even bother to sew you up? Since you are just going to leave and foolishly throw your life away?"

"You will do it because I ask, Little Father. You brought me into the Tong, trained me to be the best and the deadliest man alive. I do this not only to regain my honor but to honor you as well."

"I will help you, Lǎohǔ, but I do so with a heavy heart. You have lost your true way and I fear that you will die if you continue on this path," the old man said.

"My life is mine to throw away as I wish," Lǎohǔ said.

"That is true. Take off your shirt and lay down on the table."

~ ~ ~

"Boom, you need to take over the driving. The cops are going to be looking for me," Cooper said, pulling over to the curb.

"Why would they be looking for you?" Boom asked.

"Because I recognized one of the cops that was pulling up as we left the parking lot. His name is Jake Arnold and he's had a hard-on for my hide since I made him look like a total fool on one of my cases," Cooper explained.

"Ah, not the kind that can take a joke?"

"Not at all. He's even after the horse I rode in on."

"What the hell did the horse ever do to him?"

"Not a damn thing."

"Coop, you are one of a kind," Boom said as he slid into the driver's seat and put the van in gear. They swung by and picked up Smoke and Lindsay call.

~ ~ ~

"Where's Flipper?" Smoke asked.

"He didn't make it," Cooper said quietly.

"Well shit," Smoke said.

"Yeah," Cooper replied soberly.

"Lǎohǔ?"

"Yeah. But Flipper got lead into him before he went down."

"Good."

"So are one of you going to tell me what the hell is going on?" Lindsay Call asked.

"Lǎohǔ shot and killed Flipper. And then he got away," Cooper said, Lindsay's hands went to her mouth, her eyes wide with shock and surprise.

"Oh, Mitch!"

"Do you have enough to run your story?" Cooper asked.

"I have enough."

"Good. Then Smoke will take you to George Rain. He'll get your story out."

"What about you, Cooper?"

"I'm going to find Lǎohǔ and finish this once and for all."

"Be careful, Mitch."

"I will," Cooper told her. He hugged her tightly and kissed her long and passionately and then he let go. Call took a long moment to look into his eyes and then she turned and followed Smoke to his car.

"You sure about this, Mitch?" Boom asked.

"As sure as I have ever been about anything," Cooper told him.

~ ~ ~

"Nothing so far," Luke Santos said.

"That don't surprise me none," Jake Arnold replied.

"Why not?"

"Because Cooper is fucking connected through the Navy. The guy has people looking out for him," Arnold said.

"You sound sure of that."

"It's the truth."

~ ~ ~

Chang Chou sat quietly in the interrogation room. King and Phillips watched him through the one-way glass. "Do you believe him?" Phillips asked.

"Yeah, I think I do. Rumbles in intelligence say that the Black Dragons are at war with themselves. Different factions think that their way is the best way and they are taking out those who disagree," King told her.

"So why is this guy fixated on Mitch Cooper?" Phillips asked.

"This is pretty much conjecture on my part. I want to make sure that you realize that."

"I do," Phillips said.

"Good. Anyway, Cooper and his SEAL team went into Hong Kong after some prototype computer chips. They were ambushed at the factory and Cooper was captured. He was being tortured when his team came back for him. They got Cooper out, but not before wounding the Chinese Agent called the Tiger. Lǎohǔ blamed Cooper and swore vengeance against him. Apparently now, he has decided that it is time to collect!"

"Wow," Phillips said.

"That pretty well covers it. Except Cooper isn't the kind to just lay down and die for Lǎohǔ. And that helps account for all the goddamn bodies turning up all over San Diego," King announced.

Chapter Nineteen

"**S**o where do we start looking for Lǎohǔ?" Boom asked.

"I wish I knew right off hand. So, since I have no idea, we are going to go back to the basics," Cooper said.

"Meaning what?"

"Meaning I'm going to change my appearance and then we are going to head to Chinatown. Somebody down there might know something."

"Coop, that's Black Dragon territory. You sure that's a smart idea?"

"Probably not, Boom, but it's the only one I have."

"I don't like it."

"I'm not thrilled either, but it's the only play we have."

"We could wait for Smoke."

"We could, but that would only give Lǎohǔ more time to get away. I owe him for Flipper and Sticks. I owe him for Hong Kong. He's on my turf now, and I'm going to take him out once and for all."

"Okay, Coop, I'll back your play."

"That's all I ask," Cooper told him before going to the bedroom of the safe house to change.

~ ~ ~

"Call, what the hell are you doing here?" George Rain asked as Lindsay Call and Smoke pushed their way inside his home.

"We are still putting out at least a web edition of the paper, right?" Call asked.

"Yes."

"I've got my story for you, complete with unimpeachable sources that have been independently verified and are willing to go on the record."

"Show me!" Rain almost shouted with enthusiasm. Call put her laptop on the table and opened the file. George Rain started to read.

~ ~ ~

"Looks like you were right, Jake. This guy is a former Navy SEAL and he was on Cooper's team. I just got verification of it," Luke Santos announced.

"Good work, Luke. Any word on Cooper?" Jake Arnold asked.

"Not yet, but there is a BOLO out on him as a person of interest."

"Let's just hope the Navy doesn't squash it like they did the last time," Arnold spat out the stub of cigar. He immediately fished another one out of his pocket, stripped off the cellophane wrapper and fired the cigar up.

"You think that will really happen?" Santos asked him.

"It has before. Cooper has pull with the Navy. He's got a pet Admiral that likes to go to bat for him," Arnold waved a hand dismissively.

"Can I ask a question?" Luke asked.

"Sure."

"Why do you hate this guy so much?"

"There ain't enough hours in the day for me to answer that one," Arnold replied truthfully.

~ ~ ~

Cooper had changed to a pair of black jeans and a dark V-necked tee shirt and a black windbreaker to cover the Beretta PX-4 Storm holstered on his right hip. He had on a pair of black New Balance running shoes. A black ball cap covered his blond hair. They had swapped out the van for a blue Volkswagen Beetle. It blended in well in Historic Chinatown. Except the best place to find information would be at the *Dumpling Inn and Shanghai Saloon* at 4625 Convoy St, San Diego, CA 92111.

Cooper wanted to talk to Jimmy Han. Jimmy was a

front man for the Black Dragons as well as several other Tongs. The public face if you would. Chinese people had a problem, they went to see Jimmy Han and then the problem would be taken care of depending on whose territory that it had occurred on.

Cooper and Jimmy went way back, back to when Cooper had first started working as a private investigator. Jimmy had gotten crosswise of one of the Tongs and Cooper had managed to prove that Jimmy hadn't done what he had been accused of and had in fact been set up by a rival Tong. So Jimmy owed him.

"Wait out here," Cooper told Boom as he parked the car. He left the keys in the ignition and sighing, Boom slid over into the driver's seat. He knew that there was a better than even chance that they would be leaving in a hurry. At times, Cooper could be less than subtle when he talked to people.

Cooper entered and looked around, immediately spotting Jimmy Han. Jimmy was sitting in a corner table at the back near the doors that led to the kitchen. Cooper made a beeline for the table and had dropped into the seat across from Jimmy before the man was even aware that he had entered the restaurant. "How are you Jimmy?" he said.

"Mitchell. How have you been old friend?" Jimmy asked, his face going slightly pale.

"I've been good, Jimmy. I know an old friend is in town. I figure you might know where I might find him," Cooper replied, smiling in a way that chilled Jimmy to the bone.

"Who would that be?" Jimmy was already starting to sweat. He knew who Cooper was looking for.

"Lǎohǔ."

"You think the Tiger is in San Diego?" Jimmy asked.

"I know he is, Jimmy. I also know that there is dissension within the Black Dragon Tong. Chang Chou told me that much," Cooper told him.

"If you know all this, why don't you know where Lǎohǔ is?"

"Because he was wounded and has gone to ground. Chang Chou is singing like a canary, Jimmy. The Black Dragon Tong is finished. Lǎohǔ killed a friend of mine. I want to know where to find him," Cooper said coldly.

"I will see if I can find out and then I will call you," Han sighed.

"Be sure that you do," Cooper told him before standing up. He turned and walked away as Jimmy Han pulled out his cell phone and started making calls. Han was unaware of a bug that had been placed under the table that was recording his every word.

Cooper walked back to the car and climbed in the passenger door. "Nobody shooting at you as you leave? You losing your touch, Coop?" Boom grinned at him.

"Not at all. The Black Dragon Tong may well take the Tiger down for us," Cooper said.

"You don't really believe that do you?"

"No, but it is wishful thinking."

"I like wishful thinking."

"Yeah, me too."

"So what now?" Boom asked.

"Now we wait," Cooper told him.

"For what?"

"For word on The Tiger. Right now, Jimmy is putting out the word that I'm looking for Lǎohǔ and that he was wounded. Word is also going out about an internal battle within the ranks of the Black Dragon Tong. The other Tongs are circling, waiting to carve up their territories both here and in China."

"You know this how?"

"Because Jimmy Han is a power-broker among the Chinese in San Diego. He'll spread the word because it shows that he knows more about what is going on. That's why I chose to speak to him first," Cooper explained.

"Anybody else you want to talk to?" Boom asked.

"Not yet. I figure that in about half an hour, Jimmy is going to come out and look to see if I am still around. He'll have something to tell me if he does."

"So you plan on sitting here and waiting?"

"I do."

"You are full of surprises my friend."

"I try to be," Cooper replied.

~ ~ ~

"Call, this shit is solid gold!" George Rain said as he turned to look at his top reporter.

"I told you that when I started this story," Lindsay said.

"You did. I'm sorry I doubted you."

"So what's the verdict?"

"Upload it to the website. I don't even need to edit it. You did good, Call."

"Thanks, Boss," Lindsay beamed before she hit send.

"So who's this guy?" Rain looked at Smoke.

"One of Cooper's friends. He's been keeping an eye on me while Cooper has been going after the guy that burnt down our offices."

"Tell Cooper I said thank you," Rain said.

"I will," Smoke told him.

"Good."

"You think she'll be safe here with you?"

"Safe enough," Rain nodded.

"Then I'm going to go help Cooper end this," Smoke told them.

"Good," Rain said. He waited until Smoke had turned his back before drawing a revolver from his pocket and stabbing it toward him.

"Duck!" Lindsay screamed at the top of her lungs as she swung her purse and knocked the revolver from Rain's hand. Smoke spun, his own gun filling his fist, the muzzle pressing into George Rain's forehead.

"What the fuck is going on?" Smoke glared at Rain, his

149

finger tightening on the trigger of his gun.

"The story was never supposed to see print," Rain said, lowering his gaze to the floor.

"Then why did you hire Cooper to protect me?" Call asked.

"The Chinese wanted him out in the open so they could kill him," Rain sighed.

"And you agreed to help them?" Smoke asked his voice as soft as velvet wrapped around steel.

"The money was good," Rain shrugged.

"I should blow your fucking brains out right now," Smoke told him.

"Go ahead. I won't last in prison anyway."

"Which is why you are going to live to go there," Smoke said. He dialed Admiral Foster.

"This story needs to get out," Lindsay said.

"Then put it out there. Fuck this guy," Smoke told her.

"Oh, I will," Lindsay smiled evilly.

She immediately bent over her laptop and started typing, adding to her story before sending it out to all of the national news outlets in the country. Smoke slammed his pistol into Rain's head and dropped him to the floor.

"I'm gonna call Coop," Smoke told her.

"Do it," Call told him.

Smoke dialed Cooper's cell phone. Cooper answered.

~ ~ ~

"What?" Boom asked as Cooper answered the phone.

"Hey Smoke, what have you got?" Cooper asked.

"George Rain was working for the Chinese to draw you out," Smoke said.

"You get him?" Cooper asked.

"I did, and Lindsay has released the story on the World Wide Web. It's even fucking trending," Smoke laughed.

"Good. I'm going after the Tiger. Lindsay should be safe now that the story is out."

"Yeah, I think so too. But she wants in on the end of the story."

"I'm not sure that is a good idea," Cooper told him.

"Me either, so what do you want me to do?"

"I don't know yet."

"She's a smart Gal."

"I know that," Cooper said.

"Okay, I'll get her clear and call you back," Smoke told him. He looked down at George Rain. "You are a four-star bastard aren't you?" he asked.

"So shoot me," Rain said, grinning up at him.

"Good idea," Smoke said, firing his round into the man's head. Rain's skull exploded in a blast of red and gray. Smoke looked at Call. "You ready to Move?" he asked.

"I am. George was an asshole. I sent the story to both AP and UPI, along with sources. It will be the headline on every news station within the hour," Lindsay told him.

"Good to know," Smoke told her.

Chapter Twenty

"Your guy is leaving," Boom said.

"Follow him," Cooper said.

"So what was going on with Smoke and Call?"

"Call's boss was working for the Chinese. She quit, but she got her story uploaded to all of the major news agencies. Micro-Com is about to find itself in very deep shit and the Feds are going to be shutting this deal down and probably a number of others while the fallout happens. Don't lose Jimmy," Cooper replied.

"I don't plan to. If he can lead us to The Tiger, I'd follow him through the gates of hell," Boom replied.

"I know that. We both owe the Tiger for Flipper."

"I don't blame you, Coop, I want you to know that."

"I know, Boom."

"I'm going to miss him. He was my business partner as well as my friend."

"He was my friend and my brother too, Boom. I'll miss him as well."

"I know that, Coop." Boom sighed.

"So how about we focus on following Han and see where he takes us?" Cooper asked.

"That sounds like a plan," Boom agreed.

~ ~ ~

Lǎohǔ limped out of the house of his friend and medic. He was in a lot of pain, but he would work through that. Cooper and his men had caught him off guard at the Hotel. He could not allow that to happen again. If he did, he knew that he would die. Lǎohǔ shook his head.

Cooper was beating him and he didn't like it. It was horrible. It seemed as if the Gods themselves were against him. He had to kill Cooper and that was all there was to it.

~ ~ ~

Jimmy Han was seething. He was upset by what was happening in the Black Dragon Tong. The dissolution of the Black Dragon Tong was creating unrest and dissension among the Chinese immigrants to the United States.

He also knew that it was not Mitch Cooper's fault. Cooper was being used as an excuse by Lǎohǔ for his own actions. Jimmy Han's problem was that he needed to find Lǎohǔ and get him the hell out of the United States before the other Tongs began attacking the Black Dragon's like scavengers. The last thing needed was open war in the streets of American cities where the Tongs operated.

He was on his way to see Chin Sun, a man who was close to Lǎohǔ. Chin Sun had raised The Tiger as a boy. Jimmy knew that. He knew that Chin Sun was who Lǎohǔ would seek out. He knew that the Tiger had probably sought out Chin Sun.

Jimmy's cell phone vibrated and he pulled it out and looked at the screen. Cooper. He hit ignore and dropped it back into his shirt pocket. If he could get to Lǎohǔ and get him out of the country, then war could be averted. If Cooper caught up to Lǎohǔ, it would be a fight to the death for the two men and Jimmy had no idea which one would win.

~ ~ ~

"He's going where he thinks Lǎohǔ has gone. He ignored my call," Cooper said as Boom drove.

"That's a good thing. Because it means we'll get our shot at Lǎohǔ, right?"

"Yes. I just hope that we can take the bastard out once and for all."

"King you need to see this," Phillips said. She was at her desk at NCIS headquarters.

"What have you got?" King asked, walking behind her so he could read over her shoulder.

"Lindsay Call just broke the deal between Micro-Com and the Chinese wide open. There is no way it will be allowed to go through now."

"That is great news. But where the hell is Cooper?" King frowned.

"Where would you be if you were him?"

"I'd be going after The Tiger."

"How would he know where to do that?"

"Jimmy Han! Shit, I should have thought of him sooner!" King exclaimed. He looked at Phillips. "Come on!" Phillips jumped up and followed him towards the door.

~ ~ ~

"I must go, Little Father. The man I am after will be coming after me," Lǎohǔ said.

"Go back to China, my son. If you continue this, you may well die."

"If I die, then I die. I will meet him, but not here. You don't deserve that."

"I don't deserve to lose a son either."

"You have no say in that."

"Why, because of your honor? Why don't you honor my wishes and flee?"

"If I flee, I will always be branded a coward. I cannot live with that."

"Better to be a live coward than a dead hero, Lǎohǔ," Chin Sun snarled.

"I disagree, Little Father," Lǎohǔ shook his head.

"Of course you do. Go then. Go die for your precious honor and leave me to mourn your death."

Lǎohǔ looked at him for a long moment and then walked out the door. A car was pulling up to the curb as he stepped outside. A man climbed out. "Lǎohǔ, I am here to drive you to the airport," Jimmy Han said.

"I am not leaving yet. I have unfinished business," Lǎohǔ replied.

"If you continue to follow this foolish path, it will lead to the end of the Black Dragon Tong. Already the other Tongs are circling like wolves around a dying moose," Jimmy told him.

"The Black dragon Tong is not as feeble as you might imagine, old friend."

"You are wrong. Chang Chou has been arrested and the police are already sweeping up other members all across America, from San Diego to New York. The other Tongs and Triads are already moving in, killing or taking over the lesser members. The Black Dragon Tong is dying a fast death."

"Not for long. I will kill Mitch Cooper and then I will rebuild the Black dragon Tong in my own image! It will rise like a phoenix from the ashes and be stronger than ever!"

"I wish that could be, Lǎohǔ. I really do. But the truth is, the Black Dragons are already dead. There will be no resurrection," Jimmy Han told him.

"I am sorry," Lǎohǔ said as he drew a gun and fired, putting a bullet through Jimmy Han's brains. Jimmy hit the ground in a crumpled heap. Another car screeched to a halt and the doors flew open.

"Drop the gun, Lǎohǔ!" Mitch Cooper shouted, his Beretta already in his fist and aimed at The Tiger. Lǎohǔ smiled in the glow of the streetlight.

"We meet at last, Mitch Cooper. I will enjoy killing you."

"Dream on, Pal. I've got you covered."

"Are you afraid to meet me man to man? Or did I take your heart and courage back in Hong Kong?" Lǎohǔ smiled.

"Drop your gun and you'll get your wish," Cooper replied, twisting his head and popping his neck.

"As you wish," Lǎohǔ smiled again, kneeling down and placing his gun on the ground at his feet.

"If he wins, kill him," Cooper told Boom, laying his pistol atop the roof of the car. Cooper walked towards

156

Lǎohǔ and Lǎohǔ walked towards him. Boom watched them with sweat running down his face. He would do as Coop wished, but he didn't like it. Better to shoot the Chinese bastard and have it over with. But he knew that Cooper would never go along with that. No, he had to meet the guy one on one. But if Cooper went down, Boom wouldn't hesitate to put a bullet in the Tiger's head!

~ ~ ~

Cooper moved forward, tension leaking out of his body. He felt ready and loose as he approached Lǎohǔ. The Tiger also seemed loose and ready as they circled around each other, each waiting for the other to make the first move. Lǎohǔ jumped in a spinning back-kick which Cooper eluded and then stepped in to strike Lǎohǔ's kidney, sending the Chinese agent stumbling away from him. Lǎohǔ glared at him through slitted eyes.

"I'm waiting," Cooper grinned at him. Lǎohǔ charged, leaping into the air for a drop kick. Cooper spun out of the way and his foot struck Lǎohǔ in the back as he sailed past. The Tiger crumpled to the ground when he landed. Cooper moved in, his legs kicking out and striking the Tiger and putting him on the ground.

"I was tied to a chair the last time we faced each other, Lǎohǔ. It's a little different now that we are on even footing," Cooper taunted him.

"You will always be inferior!" Lǎohǔ screamed as he charged forward, arms and legs flashing as he attacked. Cooper parried every move and drove Lǎohǔ backward.

"It makes a big difference when your opponent fights back," Cooper said, delivering a spinning back kick that sent Lǎohǔ stumbling backward. "I could kill you at any time, Lǎohǔ. But instead, I want to humiliate you, show your people that the great Lǎohǔ is nothing more than a paper tiger," Cooper grinned.

"I am no paper tiger!" Lǎohǔ screamed, charging at

Cooper. Cooper met the charge with a kick to the throat. Lǎohǔ dropped to the ground, blood pouring out of his mouth. He couldn't breathe. Blood filled his throat as he fell into the grass. Lǎohǔ died, choking on his own blood.

"That was for Sticks and Flipper," Cooper told him as the life left his body. Sirens were growing louder as Cooper stood over the body. He would have to answer a lot of questions. He knew that. But it was over, and Hong Kong was now firmly in the past.

~ ~ ~

Two days later. Lindsay Call looked at Mitch Cooper over her coffee. "We did it," she said.

"Did what?" Cooper asked her. Boom and Shadow had already gone back to their respective homes.

"We stopped the deal, made the Chinese look bad, and saved our country."

"We did."

"You don't seem happy about it."

"I lost a friend."

"I get that. But you won, Cooper. You stopped this deal from going through. You beat the Chinese."

"Sure, I stopped them, but I lost a friend," Cooper told her.

"You gained one too," She smiled at him.

"Yes, I did."

"So where do we go from here?"

"I don't know, Lindsay. I suspect you'll move on to a bigger paper, but me? I have no idea," Cooper told her.

"I think you'll come out okay, Cooper. I know that if you ever need me, I'll always help you out."

"I appreciate that Lindsay."

"I know you will, Mitch. Don't be a stranger."

"I won't," Cooper told her. Lindsay smiled at him, and then got up and walked away, leaving Cooper to finish his coffee alone.

He lifted his cup. "To life," Mitch Cooper toasted and then he sipped his coffee once more. Life was funny that way. You never knew what tomorrow would bring, or today for that matter. You could live in the past, but to do that, you could never look to the future. The past never dies but the future is forever. Mitch knew that he needed to look to the future, no matter what in the past might beckon to him...

Thank you for reading.

Please review this book. Reviews help others find Absolutely Amazing eBooks and inspire us to keep providing these marvelous tales.

If you would like to be put on our email list to receive updates on new releases, contests, and promotions, please go to AbsolutelyAmazingEbooks.com and sign up.

Mitch Cooper Mysteries
Next in the Series

To Die For

Paloma Verdes was a woman of exotic beauty and Mitch Cooper had to admit that she had him nearly mesmerized when she first set foot in his San Diego office. But Paloma came with a sad story to go with her good looks. Her brother Enrico was a truck driver and he had taken a load up to San Clemente. She had called the company that he worked for and they had told her that he had never arrived. She wanted Cooper to locate her brother and make sure that he was okay and not dead in a ditch somewhere between San Diego and San Clemente. Cooper had known women like Paloma before, and he had learned the hard way that they weren't to be trusted. He was willing to work for her, but he didn't think that she was a woman he would be willing to die for...

About the Author

Bill Craig published his first novel at age 40 and says it only took him 34 years to become an overnight success! He has been publishing steadily ever since that first book Valley of Death and now has more books published than Carter has Little Liver Pills.

ABSOLUTELY AMAZING eBOOKS

AbsolutelyAmazingEbooks.com
or AA-eBooks.com

www.ingramcontent.com/pod-product-compliance
Lightning Source LLC
Chambersburg PA
CBHW051527050726
47503CB00014B/2059

* 9 7 8 1 9 4 5 7 7 2 1 6 0 *